M.T. ANDERSON

WALKER
BOOKS

This is a work of fiction. Names, characters, places and incidents are either the product of the author's imagination or, if real, used fictitiously. All statements, activities, stunts, descriptions, information and material of any other kind contained herein are included for entertainment purposes only and should not be relied on for accuracy or replicated as they may result in injury.

First published in Great Britain 2018 by Walker Books Ltd
87 Vauxhall Walk, London SE11 5HJ

2 4 6 8 10 9 7 5 3 1

Text © 2017 M. T. Anderson
Cover illustration © 2018 Levente Szabó
Excerpt from *Feed* © 2002 M. T. Anderson

The right of M. T. Anderson to be identified as author of this
work has been asserted by him in accordance with the
Copyright, Designs and Patents Act 1988

This book has been typeset in Dolly

Printed and bound by CPI Group (UK) Ltd, Croydon CR0 4YY

British Library Cataloguing in Publication Data:
a catalogue record for this book is available from the British Library

ISBN 978-1-4063-7900-6

www.walker.co.uk

"Funny, sad, strange and utterly brilliant. We urgently need books like this, and nobody but M. T. Anderson can write them."
Lev Grossman, author of the *New York Times* bestselling Magicians trilogy

"Resplendent with Anderson's trademark dry, sarcastic wit."
Kirkus Reviews (starred review)

"A biting and brilliant satire."
Publishers Weekly (starred review)

"Scorching, arch, hilarious and ultimately very moving."
Cory Doctorow

"Practically every word reflects a prescient, bitingly precise critique of contemporary human folly, of economic and environmental inequities and absurdities."
The Horn Book (starred review)

"A bleak but necessary lesson in trying to find the beauty in the disastrous, all while learning to recognize when it's time to dream a new dream."
BookPage

"A slim, stark, brilliant cultural commentary... This is a satirical portrait of the artist as a young man and a resonant portrait of contemporary society."
The Globe and Mail

A SMALL TOWN
UNDER THE STARS

Under the stars, a small town prepares for night. It is almost eleven o'clock. Down in the boxy houses, people are settling in for bed. Car headlights crawl through the tiny streets. The bright streetlamps on the town's main drag illuminate empty parking. The businesses are closed for the day. The hills are dark.

All of this is seen by two teens up on some ledge, on a road called Lovers' Lane.

They're parked in a fifties fin car and "necking." She's in a tight sweater; he's in a Varsity jacket. The view over their town, the place they grew up, makes them sentimental, and they grind together over the gearshift. "Gee, Brenda," says the boy.

All of this is seen by the creature in the bushes.

Stems of some kind of terrestrial growth block his goggle-eyed vision. He sweeps the branches away with a claw. He observes the two hairy snacks writhing in their metal box and wonders what their mashing together could mean. His breath is loud. With an unsteady lunge, he moves forward. Branches snap. He is on the pavement. He is beside the car.

All of this is seen by hundreds of teens, watching in horror.

Boyfriends and girlfriends squeal and lean into each other. Couples grin. They're parked in fifties fin cars and "necking." The movie screen above the field of parked cars is reflected in their windshields.

Of course, when the interstellar invasion came, it looked nothing like that.

A SMALL TOWN
AT THE FOOT OF THE
RENDERING SAILS

There is no full night in our town because the rendering sails of the vuvv stretch high into the air and glow with a dull yellow light. My girlfriend Chloe and I are lying on the grass next to the school gym, watching the sails up in the sky ripple in some invisible electromagnetic tide.

Gazing upward together, we hold hands and I say, "It's so beautiful." I think for a minute and then say, "Like your hair. Blowing."

"Adam," she says, "that's a really nice thing to say."

"Yeah," I agree, and I tilt my head so it's leaning on her shoulder. "Gee, Chloe," I say, and turn to kiss her cheek.

As it happens, Chloe and I hate each other. Still, my head is next to hers, which I would gladly, at this point, twist off with my bare hands.

All of this is seen by hundreds of vuvv, paying per minute.

THE LANDING SITE:
A STATUE OF GLASS PILLARS IN WRIGLEY FIELD, CHICAGO, ILLINOIS

I've never been to see the Vuvv First Landing Site. We all saw the landing on television when it happened, though, and for a school project in eighth grade I drew the monument that was built there on Wrigley Field. I used colored pencils and copied the picture off a cheap hologram bookmark. It was one of the first times I tried hard to draw clear glass. When I look at my drawing now, I can see a lot of the mistakes I made in getting the reflections and distortions right. The pillars look bent just because I didn't know how to do perspective well yet.

We were all surprised when the vuvv landed the first time. They'd been watching us since the 1940s, and we'd seen them occasionally, but we had all imagined them differently. They weren't slender and delicate, and they weren't humanoid at all. They looked more like granite coffee tables: squat, wide, and rocky. We were just glad they weren't invading. We couldn't believe our luck when they offered us their tech and invited us to be part of their Interspecies Co-Prosperity Alliance. They announced that they could end all work forever and cure all disease, so of course, the leaders of the world all rushed to sign up.

For a year or so after the first landing, one of their ships hovered above Wrigley Field to mark the spot where they first greeted us. Now the ship's gone, and there are luxury condos floating there instead. Everyone complains, because they block the sun, which was supposed to fall on the glass columns of the Vuvv First Landing Monument.

A few years ago, some guy in cargo pants was caught tipping over one of the monument's pillars. At first, everyone thought he was doing it as an anti-vuvv protest. Later, it turned out he was just a douche.

My House in Summer,
a '70s Suburban

Our house is half gray shingles and half brown painted panels. The shingles look okay, but all the brown panels look like hell. The paint is cracked and flaking off in long strips. What kind of dipshit would design a house half shingled and half painted? It looks confusing and it weathers unevenly.

My mom growls, "You say you want to be a painter someday. Why don't you repaint it? Pick up a brush and repaint it."

"I could, but I'm not that kind of 'painter.'"

"No, you're the irritating kind. Couldn't you be useful? You wouldn't have to repaint the shingles. You'd only have to repaint the, you know, painted parts."

I offer helpfully, "I've done landscape paintings *of* the house. I sat out there with my easel and did a whole series.

I think of them not as architectural drawings, but as studies of light on uneven surfaces."

My mother closes her eyes. "You're not doing much to keep hope alive, Adam."

"Mr. Reilly liked them. I discovered that by painting the house face-on, instead of at an angle, I can create this really cool feeling of desolation and vacancy."

"Did you include the piles of bullshit you heap in every direction?"

My mother and I blow each other kisses and go our separate ways.

Now that I am bringing in a lot of the family's money, my mom can't really complain.

We also bring in a little money by having Chloe's family living in the downstairs. Chloe's older brother works part-time at the vuvv energy rendering facility. During the days, her dad sits in the backyard, throwing my old Nerf basketball into the plastic hoop. Just like my mother, he's out of work. In the fall, he raked for us.

My mom tries to be very upbeat about her job search. "The important thing to have is hope," she tells my little sister and me. Up until the vuvv came, she was a bank teller. Since she lost her job there, she's only worked for a month or a few weeks at a time. She worked at a grocery store, restocking the Lay's. She cleaned houses with a friend of hers, until her

13

friend's list of clients shrank and there was no work left.

"You know the great thing about the job market right now?" she tells my sister and me. "Flexibility. Everything is really flexible. You have to be willing to change like *that*." She slaps one palm off the other, like it's a skipping rock. "This is a great time for entrepreneurs."

She spends the day e-mailing people résumés. That doesn't take too long, so she spends the rest of the time pacing in circles, waiting for bosses to get back to her. You can tell she paces, because the nap of the living room rug runs backward in an oval, picking its way around the convertible sofa.

A FOOD CART
IN FRONT OF A STRIP MALL,
A LINE OF CUSTOMERS

I did a sketch of a food cart where my mother was applying for a shift. She was waiting to talk to the cart's manager. I remember she jangled her keys up and down in rhythm while I drew the line of customers. "This'll be great," she said. "Restaurant jobs are hard to come by nowadays. No one's going out to eat anymore. But I have a good feeling about this." She pointed her keys at Heather's Bucket of Broth. "Everyone can afford a cup of chicken stock. This place is going to stick around. The line's a good sign. It's around the block. I think I have like a sixty/forty chance of getting the job. Maybe sixty-five/thirty-five."

I asked, "How much an hour?"

"I don't know. But I really think I can get this soup job. I can do this. I have a master's." She stared nervously at the tattooed girl who was working the window. "It's only part-time until I get something big. Like the admissions job at Qualiplay. I don't think they've filled it yet. At least, I sent them another e-mail and they didn't reply to tell me the job was filled. I have probably a thirty percent chance there. Okay, it's been a few months. Maybe twenty-five." She drew in her breath. "No, you should have seen the way that guy Brandon shook my hand after the interview. It's a solid thirty percent… Thirty/seventy. That's not so bad. Almost one in three chances. Right? I wish these people would order and get out of the way."

A guy in a business suit turned around. "We're all waiting," he said.

"Oh, no, I'm not getting broth," said my mother, laughing stiffly. "I've applied for a job. I'm just waiting to ask her if I got it."

He smiled. "Yeah," he said, "all of us are waiting to hear about the job."

I looked carefully at the other people in line. Several of them had extra résumés pinched in their fingers.

"Hey!" the broth girl shouted to all of us. "I told you guys! Get out of here! I'm picking someone tonight! Case closed. Stop all asking me!"

We looked at each other sheepishly. The line started to disperse, except a couple of people who actually wanted the bouillon and bread special.

The business suit guy was walking with us across the parking lot. "I can't believe this," he said. "I used to have a team of eleven working for me."

"Flexibility is really important right now," said my mother. "I was reading an article about how this is a great time for innovation. This is the moment for entrepreneurs."

"I actually had an administrative assistant," suit guy said. "I would give her Post-it notes with stuff I wanted her to do written on them." He held out a finger. "Here, Becky. Could you do this for me? Done."

I suspected he was trying to impress us. I wondered if there had been any Becky.

"The important thing," said my mother, "is to stay positive."

"You betcha," said suit guy dismally. "You have an extra résumé?"

"Sure. I always bring one." She pulled it out of her purse. "My son's an artist. He helped me pick the fonts."

Suit guy scanned the page. "See, this looks great. It looks perfect," he said. "What's the fucking world coming to?"

"I read an article that said that all it takes is just one good idea."

"Yeah. I like how you've formatted your skill set."

"We just have to stay positive and keep networking."

"Networking is the magic word."

We walked around the corner. We were out of sight of Heather's Bucket of Broth. That's when suit guy threw my mother against the wall.

"Listen, bitch," he said. "You're not applying for that soup job. It's mine. I have your fucking address now, and if I see you working there next week, I'm going to come over and burn your motherfucking house down." He threw the résumé into the air. "With your fucking shitty artist son still inside. Got it?" He stalked off.

The résumé spun and plunged to the ground.

We both were shaking. "I should have punched him," I said. "I can't believe it! I didn't even think of punching him! He attacked you!"

My mother steadied herself. "It was a surprise."

"I'm as tall as him."

"It was a surprise, honey. I should have punched him, too."

Now that it was over, my adrenaline was cresting. "I'm going to find him!" I said. "We have to find him! We'll call the police."

"I'm not backing out of the soup job if they give it to me," said my mother. Her voice quavered.

Throughout the evening, she kept on saying, "I'm not backing out." I think she was convincing herself. "I have a forty/sixty chance of getting that job, and I'm not backing out."

"If you get it," I said, "I'll walk you to your shifts when I'm not in school."

"I still have mace. Unless it expired. Does it expire?"

It didn't matter. My mom didn't get the job. She never heard back from Heather. A week later we passed the broth shack, and there was a sixty-year-old woman working there, hard as nails, dishing out consommé.

MY HOUSE IN WINTER

I remember the neighborhood when it looked good. People still made their yards look like something from an ad for minivans, life insurance, or weed killer. Now the neighborhood was a mess. It wasn't just that people had to get most of what they owned by scavenging. It was also that people had lost hope. Everyone spent their days trying to figure out how to get stuff for their family to eat.

Almost no one had work since the vuvv came. They promised us tech that would heal all disease and would do all our work for us, but of course no one thought about the fact that all that tech would be owned by someone and would be behind a paywall. The world's leaders met with the vuvv, after meeting with national Chambers of Commerce and various lobbyists. The vuvv happily sold their knowledge to captains of industry in exchange for rights to the Earth's electromagnetic energy fields and some invisible quantum events. Next thing we knew, vuvv tech was replacing workers all over the world. At first, it was just manual labor, factory labor. Show tech a product – a shirt, a swing set, a subdivision – and in minutes tech could make it from trash. No reason for an assembly line, for workers. We watched a billion people around the globe lose their jobs in just a year or two. My parents thought they were safe, white-collar.

My mom was a bank teller. Most of her work was already done by ATMs, even before the vuvv came, and what was left required someone who could listen, think, decide, and verify. But within six months of the vuvv landing, she was fired. Almost all bank tellers were fired, and so was everyone else who did paperwork and customer interface in any other business. Vuvv tech did it all now – a computerized voice purring, "Let me help you with that"; "I'm sorry, but your account is already overdrawn"; "Very funny, Mr. Costello. I always appreciate a little sarcasm at day's end."

The human economy collapsed. No human currency could stand up against the vuvv's ch'ch. The lowliest vuvv grunt made more in a week than most humans made in two years. Only the wealthiest of humans could compete, once they had a contract for vuvv tech, once they could invest in vuvv firms.

My father thought that his job was safe. He was a Ford salesman. There was no way, he said, that he could be replaced by a computer, because salesmen need that human touch, that twinkle in the eye. It turned out, however, that no one could afford a new car anyway. With the human economy in the shitter, who had the money to upgrade just to get a Ford Desperado that could run errands for Mom on its own, pick up a dozen donuts from the drive-thru and a bottle of Pepto? Sales were nil. People were holding on to their dumb mouth-breather pre-AI plastic sedans. He was one of the best salesmen, but the showroom let him go. He was laid off. He couldn't believe it. He said he was not just a car, truck, and recreational vehicle salesman – he was selling the American dream. But our leaders were making speeches about how America's middle class had to stop dreaming and start learning how to really work. By that point, I'm not sure there really even was a middle class anymore – just all of us hoeing for root vegetables next to our cracked aboveground pools.

People always need food – many tried to turn to farming, and in the shattered suburbs, people grew their lawns into paddocks, chicken yards, and plots. But the vuvv could grow food cheaper, and their government subsidized it, and that meant they could sell it cheaper, and, frankly, our family had almost no money, so when we went to the supermarket, we didn't buy American; we almost always bought vuvv-grown veggies, vuvv cereal, beef tissue raised on platforms in orbit (the cow jumped over the moon). Farms failed. Economies collapsed. Only big industrial farms that could act as distributors for vuvv foodstuffs stayed viable.

The only way to make money was to work with the vuvv personally. Work as a technician at a vuvv firm and you could make a few hundred dollars a week. Go into the tourist industry, give the vuvv a massage, and you made several hundred dollars in an hour. Stand at attention for three hours at a vuvv banquet – nothing but show, of course – and you'd make enough to live on for a year. People killed, literally, to get close to the vuvv. They killed to get property rights to vuvv resorts and locations for energy rendering plants.

In one of my paintings of my family's house, my father is sitting on the stoop with his head on his knees. It couldn't have been an easy pose, but I just found him that way.

"I can't provide," he said.

I shrugged. "No one can."

"I've been everywhere. No one anywhere has work. I think of those Iranian heart surgeons you used to run into driving cabs in New York. Now there aren't even cabs." We had eaten almost nothing but instant mashed potatoes for a week.

"It's not your fault," I told him, trying to sketch the hairy shanks of shingles.

He looked up at our two cars, his and Mom's, both of

23

them pretty new – his car eager and ready at the drop of a hat to navigate a family trip to San Antonio or even just run out to grab us some charcoal for the grill. "I got those with my discount," said Dad. "I got a great price on them."

"I know you did."

"It made sense for us to have two cars."

"Dad, you'll get another job."

"I knew the inside and outside of that business."

I could tell how much it hurt him to talk about this. I just nodded.

He said, "Do you think I'm not a man, because I can't find work?"

"Dad, that's stupid," I said. "That's just dumb gender stuff."

A year and a half later, I still don't know what it means to "be a man." But I do know what it means to be a coward.

My Parents' Bedroom, with the Covers Askew

(Charcoal on paper)

In the charcoal picture of my parents' room drawn just after my father disappeared, the bed looms large. The sheets are still yanked around from when my father got up. My mother's bathrobe is lying on the floor. My father's shoes are all over the place. Each of my parents has a bedside table. On my father's is a spy thriller that he must have been reading. On my mother's is a statuette of an inhumanly long ballerina. My sister's leg is in the picture, coming in from the side.

I drew it while we were sitting there. I put in Nattie's leg because I wanted the room to feel empty but watched by someone unseen.

We had not heard from my father for two days when I drew the picture. My mother was sleeping in the living room while Nattie and I sat there, looking at his abandoned things.

My mom knew he had left suddenly, loudly, in the middle of the night. He just got up from bed and banged the closet door open, tore off his T-shirt, flung it on the ground, and got dressed.

"What's going on?" she asked him. She was still half-asleep.

He snapped, "Charity auction," and left.

When I drew the picture, I assumed he had gone off somewhere hidden, alone and pathetic, and committed suicide. We were worried that the police would find his car abandoned and his body nearby.

The picture is a study in slats. The only light comes through the Venetian blinds and leads in strips across the rucked covers, the comforter. My hands, I remember, were black with charcoal.

A day later we discovered it was worse than suicide: my father had just fled. He had taken his car – the more expensive one, of course, the one with the self-steering synaptics – the newish car that we could have sold for five months' worth of food – and he'd run away from his own kids to save himself. The fucker was in some other state. He didn't say where. He sent us a group message. It included the information that he loved us.

He said that he didn't feel like a man anymore. That being bullshit, I decided that, sure, he was not a man anymore, but in a different sense than he meant it: he was a ghost, a spirit. Whatever he did now was not real. He could haunt Montana or shack up in the mountains of Southern California. But it was not my father who did these things. It was a coward, a fume, a fugitive who was less than human.

This is one of my first charcoals. I'm left-handed, so most of it is too smudged to see. I dragged the shade across the whole page. The hand that records is also what makes everything unclear.

A Dining Room,
Empty Except for Light

Our dining room, like many dining rooms, is set up to represent a world where people dine together. There is a table, and it has six chairs. Six people could gather to eat there, theoretically. I don't know who they would be, except maybe a family back in the 1980s, exchanging lively stories of their day over Hamburger Helper and green beans before going off to watch wholesome sitcoms about other families who eat dinner around dining room tables, but with a laff track guffawing every time the cute toddler finger-guns and moonwalks.

We certainly never used the dining room. For most of my childhood, it just sat there, waiting for a perfect evening that never happened. Dining rooms are the vermiform appendix of American architecture. They're left over from some earlier phase of evolution, and everyone still has one, even though we no longer need them to digest.

In my painting of the dining room, I try to capture how empty it is. Somehow, having a big table and six chairs in the room, instead of filling the space, makes it more empty. On the walls, there are pictures of us, so my painting is a picture of pictures. There's a pastel portrait of my grandmother that was done in New York by a street artist, which makes her look like she had a broken jaw. There are several digital and holographic frames that rotate through family photos. My father is still in the rotation. He appears sometimes, smiling and standing on a dock in Newport. Then he fades, and there we all are in Texas or Wyoming. While I was painting my picture of the dining room, I realized that for several months, one of our digital frames had been broken and no one had noticed. It was blank. It had stopped broadcasting our faces, as if it had just given up on us and shut its eyes. I painted it gray, with the sheen from the window reflected on its screen. The other frame kept beaming our grins, showing off our family to an audience of no one.

I had a choice, which picture to include in my painting. I chose a picture of my father and me playing basketball in front of the house. We're both leaping.

The night the Marshes came to live with us, Mom ordered me to set the table in the dining room. She said we would have a little "meet and greet."

I took the woven place mats in and lay them around the table. I didn't even argue with her. I had seen Chloe Marsh earlier in the day – very pretty, with a face shaped like a soft heart and with a delicate nose and lips like a contessa in a Renaissance portrait. The last thing I wanted was this new pretty girl, who was going to be living with us, to hear me getting yelled at through the floor. I picked up a handful of knives, forks, and spoons, counting us out: my mother, my twelve-year-old sister Nattie, and me, then three Marshes. I circled around the table, laying down flatware.

Nattie came into the room with her back pressed against the wall like a commando on a black ops mission. She slid toward me and whispered, "Have you seen them?"

I nodded. "When they were moving their stuff in."

"The older brother?" She made a tragic grimace that puckered her chin. "How old do you think he is?"

"Twenty. Twenty-one."

"He looks like his face was made to spit." She suddenly realized what I was doing. She asked in bewilderment, almost disgust, "Why are you setting the *dining room table*?"

"This is where we're eating."

"Don't be weird."

I shrugged. "It's what Mom said."

"We can't. This room has a dark, broken soul. It would be like eating in an Egyptian tomb."

"Hey: I was thinking of hanging my painting of the dining room in here. In the dining room."

"Don't, Adam. Don't. It'll create an infinite vortex, and we'll fall in and never come out."

I laughed; she stared at me solemnly. Then she went through to the kitchen and said, "Mom. We're not eating in the dining room."

"Yes, we are. The Marshes are new."

"That's why we can't have them in the dining room. We've never tested it."

When the three Marshes came upstairs, my mom had put out rice and beans. We ate rice and beans most nights. Either rice and beans or rice and lentils. It was cheap.

The Marshes stood awkwardly in the kitchen and stared at the pot of rice and the pot of beans. The Marsh brother, Hunter, was staring at the food so hard I got creeped out.

Marsh Dad said, "This is really nice of you, Mrs. Costello."

"Yeah," said Hunter, and he moved to the stove like a predator and started spooning himself out dinner. "Should we just start?" he said. "Where's the silverware?"

"I thought we'd eat in the dining room," said my mother cheerfully. "We'd like to welcome you into our home."

The dining room was terrible. We either sat up straight in our chairs or hunched down close over our plates. Chloe Marsh was trying to look at nothing but her food. After I knew her better, I realized that she was probably feeling embarrassed that night. They had just come to town a couple of days before, bringing almost nothing. They were used to having their own house, their own yard. Now they only had a van of furniture.

"Where are you moving from?" my mother asked, to make conversation.

"Upstate New York," said Mr. Marsh. "Near Syracuse."

"Oh, nice!" my mother exclaimed.

"It's a wasteland," said Mr. Marsh. "I was an idiot not to get out of there sooner. This billionaire sold off a lot of the land near us to some company to build a vuvv triplex gathering hole. I didn't sell. I was like, 'Screw that.' We had this house with a pool, almost an acre. Everyone said the vuvv hole meant big business was coming to town. The whole area was going to boom. Our place was supposed to be worth almost a million." His mouth was full of beans. "For about two years, it probably was. Worth a million. Then everything started to go to shit."

"Dad," Chloe warned.

"No, it did. Oh, sorry, the little one." He pointed his knuckle at Nattie. "But you've heard how it is near the holes. There was ashes in the air all the time. Disgusting. Everything started to die and turn into glass." He chomped a few times. "No one's moving there. Everyone's getting out as fast as they can. Last week I finally sold. To the company that's running the gathering hole, of course. For a dollar. A goddamn dollar."

We all chewed for a while. Hunter played with his phone. With Chloe sitting there, I didn't want to chew, because I thought the squelching would be too loud. I didn't want her to look at me at all. I felt too awkward being in the room with her. I wished my arms could fold up in more places so I would take up less room.

"We have a vuvv rendering plant near here," said my mother. "Should I be worried?"

"No. No. Hunter has a job at the rendering plant. That's why we're here. It's completely different from a triplex gathering hole. Totally."

Hunter, still staring at his phone, announced, "Your connection sucks ass."

Mr. Marsh said, "Hunter."

"I wasn't meaning it mean," said Hunter. "Just factual. It sucks ass."

Mr. Marsh asked, "What do... What do you do, Mrs. Costello?"

My mother smiled weakly. "I'm sort of between... Just, well, waiting to hear back from a couple of prospective..." She didn't finish. We all kept eating. I know every one of us hated being in the dining room. Spiritually, we all were sitting on the corduroy furniture in the living room, and we had never come in here at all, we had never made the terrible choice to eat together with the picture frame flashing its scenes of vacations in the Great Lakes region or of Dad, Mom, Nattie, and me grinning like goobers, dressed up in Pilgrim clothes. This meal would be silent and would never end.

Then Chloe turned to Nattie. "Hey, do you go to the high school?" she asked, like we were having a normal conversation. Nattie said no, she was only in eighth grade. Chloe kept asking her questions. She made my little sister feel important ("What are the schools like around here?" "What do you do to have fun?"), and this was when I realized that Chloe was not just beautiful but kind and thoughtful.

After dinner Chloe said she would put the dishes in the dishwasher. I said I would help her. Hunter went off without saying anything – thank you or good-bye – stomping back downstairs until his father screamed, *"Hunter? Hunter! Say thank you to Mrs. Costello, for fuck's sake."*

In the stunned silence that followed, Hunter said something miserable and then kept sinking into the shadows. My mother was agape.

Chloe brought the plates in from the table, and I rinsed them and put them in the dishwasher.

"Sorry about that room," I whispered. "It's not a good place."

She touched her heart. "Oh my god," she said. "I thought it was only me. But there's a curse, right?"

"People have got to get rid of dining rooms. Every one of us."

"That's the last of the glasses." She put two down next to the sink.

"If you're interested," I said, "I can show you around tomorrow. The high points. The important features of the landscape."

"Here," she said. "What do we do with napkins?"

PORTRAIT OF CHLOE SEATED IN A GARDEN

The first time I ever painted Chloe, I tried to do it in the style of the Renaissance masters. I had sketched her a few times in the first week she was living with us, and the third week, I used those sketches to paint a whole scene with her in it. I am no idiot: painting someone's portrait is a goddamn love magnet. It gives you time to talk to them and flirt, to really get acquainted, and they're flattered; and meanwhile, you're getting to know their face, to love its angles and its proportions.

I based the portrait on the Old Master pictures of saints Mr. Reilly showed me where the holy undead are in a magical garden. In those paintings, angels cluster around the living and the dead who sit peaceably on thrones, making signs with their hands. Just outside the garden walls is regular life, there are normal streets with dogs and puddles, and merchants and money changers go about their business, and farmers are working in the fields, but inside those hidden, holy spaces, these solemn people are outside of time. They are beyond hurt, beyond wounding.

I painted Chloe sitting on a throne in a dress of burnished gold, surrounded by flowers.

Outside the walls of her secret garden, it is our town, with rain falling on houses in rows and on the distant, metal towers of the vuvv. But the sun falls on Chloe. Angels bow on either side of her, offering her Hostess CupCakes and hot pizza bites and sliders.

She went kind of crazy when she saw it. "Oh my god! Oh my god! That is hilarious! That's the best!" I didn't point out that I'm not good at faces.

We started going out a few weeks after her family moved in. At first, it was super sexy, figuring out that she was into me when we bumped elbows getting stuff down from shelves; it was even sexier when I was painting her, and each stroke of the brush across the cheek on the board felt to us both, I think, like a caress; and the best was when we finally told each other, and we had to sneak around and keep it from our parents, her brother, and my little sister. We giggled silently behind the sofa while her dad shouted at the television: "Blow their damn heads off!" and "Yeah, baby! You're the one for me!" Chloe had to drive her fingernails into my thigh to stop me from snorting out loud with laughter.

We went on scavenging trips together in the shadow of the floating houses in Barrington. We hoped we could find some furniture or something to sell. The weird thing about the rich, though, is that when they're done using something, they don't want anyone else using it either. They want their trash to be trash. As if having a sofa in a house on the ground taints its history in a house up in the sky. As if we, down on the ground, would pull one of their fancy pre-vuvv stereo amps out of the garbage heap and somehow claw our way back along the cord, shimmying up it into the clouds and climbing into their living rooms, fee-fi-fo-fum.

At that point, it didn't even matter that Chloe and I were often standing knee-deep in piles of garbage and filth in the shadow of rich-people floating houses. We were in love.

A Crystal City
in a Range of
Misty Mountains

When I was thirteen and fourteen, I loved making landscapes on GameFury Cyberplatz. I made them 3-D. I wanted to someday be an artist for VR environments, create the spaces where you jump in free fall and spin and fire into surprising gulfs. I designed landscapes like this crystal city holospace – fantasy spots that never could exist – and I thought about what looked cool and unexpected, where the hidden doors could be, where you could roll, where it made sense to turn around and look backward, and where the ambush would hide.

Mr. Reilly was my art teacher in high school. He tried to convince me to paint using paint. It seemed like a weird thing to do, so I refused at first, except when ordered to. He would show me the Old Master paintings of saints being killed in ancient orchards or angels having some kind of feast on cloth of gold, surrounded by ruins, and he pointed out to me that these were the fantasy landscapes of yesteryear. I didn't care about the saints, but I was fascinated by the castles perched on distant hills, the towns on outcroppings with switchbacks leading up to them, the ruins in the shadows. I made them into game worlds.

I guess it was after my father left that I started to paint them using paint. It was strange.

"Why do you use paint to paint?" Chloe asked me, as I worked on copying a saint picture. I was concentrating on the image and my piece of board, but our legs were tangled up together. She said, "Paint is so old shkool. It's like wearing garters to hold up your socks."

I shrugged. "I guess I want to make something that's actually in the world. Instead of just seeming to be real when you have on the right helmet."

"Hmm," said Chloe. "Like love."

"Whoooaaaa," I said, drawing it out. We laughed.

"You're this amazing artist," said Chloe, "but, yeah, you kind of missed a big part of the picture."

"What do you mean?"

"You missed the guy with the arrows in him. In a picture of a guy with arrows in him."

"I don't care about the guy," I said. "I just like the house way back there on the cliff. That's where I want to be. Away from where things happen. In a hidden house that looks out on everything."

Because we thought we were in love, she said, "Can I have my own set of keys made?"

And I said, "You'll have your own gate and garden."

My House in Early Fall
(Watercolor on paper)

When I did a painting of the house in early fall, the leaves were just starting to turn. I painted the trees as bright streaks of red. They actually looked vibrant in my painting, because I was happy that day. Things were going well with Chloe. We had come up with a plan to make our families money.

We had been hanging out for a couple of months when she heard about the hookups. The name was a pun. Couples in love were hooking themselves up to some vuvv tech and transmitting the whole experience to the vuvv.

The vuvv budded. They didn't need partners. They didn't have sexes. There was no evolutionary reason for them to ever invent romance. Instead, they were big on family ties: parent, spawn.

For humans, there was a good biological reason to enjoy

sunsets and long walks on the beach, candlelight on the mistletoe. It aided in reproduction and in convincing both parents to stay around and fight for their scrawny, helpless young. For the vuvv, there was none of that. Each parent had to protect their brood alone and provide something for the future. This, they say, is why they're such incredible businessthings.

"It's new to them," said Chloe. "Holding hands. They pay to watch humans in love. It would be fun."

I was horrified at first.

"Like porn?" I said.

She thought about it uncomfortably. "But love," she said. "1950s love. That's what they want. That's what they saw from their saucers, so that's what they think we do."

"You're saying we'd be hooked up to some tech, and then I'd take you out for a chocolate malt at the drugstore and say, 'Gee, Chloe.'"

"Exactly."

"That's it? Sweet nothings?"

"You're so funny," she said, grinning. "Exactly." She bopped my nose with her finger.

"We're so cute! We would've made six dollars just now."

"Six-fifty because of your eyebrows."

Needless to say, 1950s-dating someone you live with is a huge mistake.

Us Running
Hand in Hand
Through Grasses,
Maybe Wheat

I designed a site with us running hand in hand through some kind of field. It's cartoony, so we're more adorable. If you wait for a minute, it switches to a thing where we're on opposite sides of the space, and we run toward each other with our arms out. Then, as we collide, our bodies turn into a burst of flowers and spray through each other. The flowers drift and spell out "Ad & Chloe." Then you can choose episodes.

"Why are we standing in so much grass?" Chloe asked with her arm around my neck. "Aren't we worried about ticks?"

"Maybe it's wheat," I said. "Wheat's nostalgic. As a crop."

"You have some weird ideas."

"Wheat's super American."

"Do they even grow wheat around here? Where do they grow wheat now?"

I shrugged. "Floating around the sun, mainly."

Each episode was one of our dates. We went to a party where I introduced Chloe to people from my school, or we baked snickerdoodles, or we just hung in a parking lot. Each episode had a little title and a description translated into vuvv. "Ocean Memories: Humans Adam and Chloe are going to the beach now! They are in true love. They have playful splashing. The water is too cold for organism Adam and he squeals like a piggy, says loving Chloe! Humans find the oscillating presence of hundreds of billions of gallons of a chemical that could smother them relaxing. This leads to cuddles in mounds of finely ground particulate detritus. 'I'll always be true,' says Adam!"

We got dressed up specially for our dates. There was a real feeling of excitement, at first. Chloe put on special skirts; I put on a special shirt. I would pass Chloe in our bathroom, stretching out one of her eyes and dabbing it with an applicator. There were tubes and cans of products all around the sink. She would slam the door shut playfully. While she was in the bathroom, I got ready for our date by taping the sensors onto my heart and skull. They picked up what we heard, saw, and smelled and recorded it for the site. When we were ready to go out, we whispered a quick "Go, team!" to each other, and then strapped the translation boxes onto our chests. The vuvv speak by grinding a sort of gritty fin against their body, so most of what we said, translated, sounded like sandpaper or, when we were shouting, Velcro.

We headed out into the summer night, ready for adventure.

We went to Austin's house and watched a horror holo. As the deranged phys ed teacher stripped the muscles off his prize athletes and tied them to his own limbs like a bloody bikini, all of us screamed, and Chloe and I leaned together and seized each other's knees. Apparently, our vuvv customers were fascinated. Why is the sight of torture, a glimpse of some flayed bull-jock dying under the bleachers, erotic? Why do we seek out fear?

Another evening, we took Nattie out for ice cream. Chloe and I were proud of the money we had coming in, so it was our treat. We bought her a cone.

As evening fell, we hung out on a median strip, counting padiddles – cars with one headlight burnt out. It wasn't a perfect date – lots of exhaust in our cookies 'n' cream – but the vuvv love customs.

"A whole lot of padiddles," said Chloe, and Nattie said, "They always remind me of tomcats with one eye out from a street fight. Don't they look like they're prowling?"

Chloe laughed and said it was great Nattie had such a good imagination.

I was proud of both of them, and I said so, and I heard the scratching of the box on my chest as it was translated.

It was recorded for "Ice Cream Memories."

We were always aware that our love had an audience. There were vuvv subscribers, some live, some watching stuff cached, and even some of the kids at school tuned in. I would be walking down the hall at school and a complete stranger going the other direction would extend his hand to give me five.

As we went shopping for bulk foods or kicked sand at the beach, we were always thinking about the invisible viewers who hovered around us like a band of watchful angels. So we laughed louder, we kissed longer, we tried to say smarter stuff, hesitating a second to think up the best gag. It's like we were ringed by cherubim, smiling at our antics. It made everything more real.

We watched the number of our subscribers go up, and that made us even more giddy when we were together. We'd think of romantic scenes from movies and try to play them out, climbing out on the roof to look at the stars. Neither of us knew shit about astronomy, but: *Look, we're lying side by side, hand in hand. We're the perfect couple!* I got total asphalt-burn from the shingles.

I could not believe I had scored someone like Chloe – so thoughtful and beautiful, as she seemed to me at first. When she was in a bathing suit, it was like nothing else existed in the world. We sat there by my friend Brad's pool, which unfortunately was filled with rainwater, algae, and peepers, and

I could hear my friends talking, but I couldn't pay attention, because I was looking at Chloe's soft limbs and thinking that I was allowed to touch them whenever I wanted.

I was devilishly seductive, but when it came to romantic evenings, I had certain drawbacks – for example, let's put the cards on the table, I have Merrick's Disease, a stomach syndrome I caught from our untreated tap water – as part of the vuvv's austerity measures, municipal water is no longer purified – so I'm frequently tortured by gas, diarrhea, and let's say "distress," which covers a whole host of pains and eruptions. It's something I have to be aware of when I'm out on the town. A lot of people were suffering from this kind of thing, and I had it particularly bad.

But there we were, lying side by side on a towel in a world that, between the leeches in the sludgy pool and the greasy storm in the pit of my stomach, seemed deeply stained and mucky – but she was a perfect shape beside me, clean as vanilla.

Soon we had a lot of vuvv subscribers. We were making hundreds of dollars a month. After we recorded an episode, we sat whispering in her room, talking about what we could have done better and how to expand our viewer base.

I did some slang research. "I should say more things like, 'Golly, you're marvelous!'"

"You could call me a 'solid sender.'"

"I don't know what that is, but you are it, strongly."

"I really am."

"You're dynamite."

I built her a castle in VR. It became a date episode, "Fun in a Love Fortress!" I gave her an avatar and I led her into the great hall, and showed her all the spaces I made for her. There was a tapestry with her surrounded by flowers, and there was a museum with statues of all of her childhood pets. (I asked for photos.) She couldn't believe how much work I'd put into the castle for her. Outside the castle window, it was summer and she had her own lake, and there was a stone library for her with a big Renaissance-y window. Deep within the castle, there was a dungeon I called the Pit of Id, which was a murky place with thin staircases leading through dank air. They went to little grottoes where there were games I'd set up for her, fun little things I'd found all over the net and stowed away for her to while away the hours – battle games, dumb apps where you would try to grab all the clams and oysters on the ocean floor before you were eaten by a shark, links to cute little monster sims. She laughed and leaned into my virtual shoulder and said, "You are such a *nerd*," but it sounded nice, just then.

It didn't sound so nice a month later. I'd been adding more rooms on for her, trying to work around hints I got of things she liked. It was tough, because she didn't really have any hobbies or specific interests. We had a lot of dates where we visited the virtual castle. And it was bad, because when I'd lead her to the new rooms – a cat stable, a karaoke chapel – I could tell she was a little restless. "Oh, honey," she said, "this is so nice!" But it didn't sound really sincere. It sounded like she was putting it on for the cloud of vuvv who watched us.

During our whispered conference after one flat session, I said, "During the tour of the castle, you didn't look interested in the new rooms. It would be better if you looked interested in stuff I do for you." I explained carefully: "More romantic."

"Oh, sorry," she said. "I'm just..."

"What's wrong?"

"Well, I like your make-believe stuff—"

"Virtual reality, yeah."

"But I wish we went *actually* out more. The fake castle's nice, but I want to meet more people from school."

"We went to a party a couple of weekends ago."

She agreed dully. "Okay."

I didn't want to push the party too much, because honestly it seemed like she wasn't as interested in my friends as she was in some other kids. I was worried that she was headed for a different crowd. I didn't really want to talk about it with her, though, because I was afraid I might be right.

So we avoided each other's eyes that night, and we didn't even kiss before I went back upstairs. Through the air ducts, I heard her whispering to someone over a link: a friend from back home, maybe, or someone she'd met at school.

I sat on my bed, hearing the murmuring through the floor. My stomach was in an uproar. It felt like all the tubes led to one central place in which something evil sat, stewing.

A Small Town
Beneath a Hovering
Luxe Cloud Complex

I painted the vuvv anti-gravity lobes and the towers and hanging vanes of a rich-people cloud-complex after Chloe and I visited one. It was the only time I'd ever gotten to see my own town from above, so I painted that, too, in the landscape under the complex. You can see the town's rendering sails, but also the Catholic church steeple and the rows of 1960s suburbans falling into disrepair.

I wanted Chloe to meet Mr. Reilly before school started, but he spent most of his days up in the air. Teaching art at the high school was just volunteer for him. He did it out of the good of his heart. No one was paying for art in schools. Most of the time he worked as a doorman at one of the floating apartment buildings of the wealthy. It was chic to have an actual living person you could order around. He stood there all day saying, "Thank you, sir. A pleasure to see you, Ms. Notrevka." Vuvv tech could have done it better than him, but, as he said, he was a luxury item. He hated the job but was glad he had it.

Mr. Reilly arranged for us to go up on a cargo lift, sitting on crates of frozen potatoes gratin. He met us at the service elevator. He treated Chloe like she was a visiting princess, bowing and shaking her hand. She laughed and thought he was cool. We sat with him behind his desk, looking out the huge windows at the town spread beneath us.

"The rendering sails look so tiny!" said Chloe.

Mr. Reilly pointed out, "You can see the ocean from here."

When a rich person entered the lobby, we fell silent out of respect and didn't look at them. Mr. Reilly greeted them pleasantly and gave them messages, even though they must all have been ringed and tingling with media that could deliver updates much more reliably than the old-world tech of a mouth and teeth, a guy in epaulets and gold-braided pants.

Mr. Reilly said, "Show me what you've been working on," and I called up a hologram of Castle Chloe. It hung all around us. "This is great!" said Mr. Reilly, soaring through it. "See, the irregularity of the small turret coming out of the big tower – it provides some real architectural interest and a break in the regularity of the scale. And the stone surfaces are really convincing. You must have found a great algorithm for cut stone." He shifted a few inches forward and back. "Perfect. Look at how it behaves in the torchlight. That's perfect."

Chloe smiled at me and I smiled at her and Mr. Reilly smiled at both of us. At that moment, I wished I could elect Mr. Reilly as my grandfather. Maybe even my father, if he'd agree to pull the polyester lint off his necktie.

I was showing him around the castle pleasure gardens, which bobbed around us, when a bunch of rich kids came into the lobby from the garage. They were dressed in high-end clothes like unclamped, casual vacuum suits, because that was the big thing in the fashion world, looking like you were about to carelessly jet off to another solar system, tra-la-la, and by noon tomorrow you'd be sitting at a resort under two suns, slamming back an oxygen-rich atmosphere mix with an alien hedge-fund manager who was nothing but a heap of intelligent lichen.

"Hi, kids!" said Mr. Reilly, giving them his big doorman smile.

The kid in the lead – a couple of years younger than me, maybe fifteen, a boy who looked like he'd been chiseled specially to play lacrosse at Yale – he was pulling some kind of new appliance in a huge cardboard box on an anti-grav dolly. He parked it by the wall and, pointing, said to Mr. Reilly, "Yeah. Dave. This." Thumb-jerk up. "Apartment 723."

My stomach shrank.

I hadn't known Mr. Reilly's name was Dave. I didn't know it because I never would have called him by his first name.

Mr. Reilly glanced at me, and I could see he was blushing. Chloe looked like she wanted to drip through a drain in the floor and rain down to Earth.

But then one of the kids in the group saw the weird angles in the flowering chasm that floated holographically around us. "Whoa!" she said. "That's ch'ch!" They came over to inspect my castle keep.

"This is Chloe and Adam," said Mr. Reilly. "They're visiting from the SkyWay complex down in Hartford," he lied kindly, as if we were other rich kids here in the foyer waiting for our rich aunt. Our clothes told another story.

The kids gaped at my creation. Chloe said shyly, "He made it for me." For a minute, it was like the castle was important to her again.

"That's so romantic," said one of the girls.

"Look at this," said Chloe, and started to show them around, even though she'd complained about trudging its corridors just a couple of days before.

I couldn't have been happier.

What am I saying? I was terrified too, at the same time. As Chloe and I walked them around the hologram battlements, Mr. Reilly stepped over to the dolly and carted off the kid's new toy or appliance or whatever to apartment 723. I was sure at any moment they were going to smoke us out and figure we were rabble, living on top of one another in a seventies junkbox down below. For one thing, we couldn't understand a word they were saying, since it was all private jokes and wealthy early-adopter sub-vuvv prep-school-blazer blather.

"Ty-Ty! Shtell! Check the king bed! Shtellooor!" (It was a great bed, I have to admit. A four-poster with griffon tapestries.)

"Shtell? Stch."

"You musta had total sys calm after you broke this to her."

I smiled broadly. "Yes, I did indeed," I agreed, hoping I wasn't agreeing to anything too awful.

"And cap your rocks!"

"Cap your ROCKS."

At one point, they asked, "What school you go to?"

No idea of the names of any rich-person schools. A blank. I smiled to gain time. Then I answered smoothly, "St. Photon's. In, um, you know, Connecticut."

"You row? You guys go to Quinsig?"

"Not a rower," I said. "Sorry!"

Chloe grabbed my arm. She wanted to be dating a big deal. "Oh, he's a long-distance runner," she bragged. "Varsity."

"Me too!" said a kid. "St. Photon's in the ISL?"

I clucked and gave a regretful shake of the head. "You

wouldn't have seen me. I damaged my Achilles tendon," I explained, squeezing Chloe tight, "when I was kneeing a complete idiot in the gut."

Luckily, they were getting excited about some of the stupid little games in the Pit of Id.

For twenty minutes, we explored my castle in the air together. They loved it. Then Mr. Reilly said it was time for us to catch our shuttle, and so I shut up the image and we both slapped our new pals in some way they seemed to want us to slap them. They said they'd see us around and to buzz 723 if we were ever "back in their sky."

Mr. Reilly led us out to the garage, as if we were going to catch a luxury shuttle, and then quickly walked us through a service door back to the cargo platform, which was ready to drop.

"You didn't have to do that," I whispered to him.

Mr. Reilly grinned. "I thought you'd like to see what an audience thought of your work!"

Chloe said, "That was the best twenty minutes of my life." Her eyes were sparkling.

"They would hate us," I said. "If they met us on the ground, they'd hate us."

"Why? We pulled it off!"

"Until they look up whether St. Photon's is in the ILR."

"The ISL."

57

"Sure. That."

"Don't ruin the day for me."

I shrugged. Mr. Reilly ("Dave") looked nervous.

The guy driving the cargo platform told us to step aboard, step aboard, ladies and gents. We both shook Mr. Reilly's hand, then the door closed and we dropped away from him, leaning our backs against garbage cans, falling toward Earth as if we weighed a million pounds.

I looked out a window. There it all was, my first eighteen years at a glance: streets and sails and shattered Stop & Shop. Sometimes you think a view from above will give you a sense of mastery and power; then it turns out it just makes you realize how small your life really has been.

MY HOUSE IN LATE FALL

By the time I painted my house in late fall, Chloe and I pretty much couldn't stand the sight of each other. We were seeing way too much of each other. All day, every day, and most of the nights. I had to listen to her freaking out at her brother. It was like she'd tantrum. She was insane. And there we both were in the kitchen every morning, looking goopy.

And I guess I wasn't a pretty package either. There's the Merrick's Disease, and the noises Chloe heard through the bathroom door obviously disgusted her. Gas, groaning, passing bloody stool. I can imagine what she was telling her new friends.

"It's a disease," I said. "What should I do?"

At first, she answered with an uncomfortable smile.

One time when the air was particularly eggy, she

suggested, "Lepers used to carry bells to warn people they were coming."

I've tried to get some kind of medicine to help with it – the vuvv can apparently solve this kind of thing in five minutes – but we have minimum insurance coverage. All the medicine in the world won't help if you don't own it. I was saving up for a single visit with a vuvv doc. I hoped I'd have enough cash by the time my small intestine shriveled like an earthworm on hot pavement.

As cool as it had been, when we were in love, to broadcast that love everywhere, as if we were stars or models, once we didn't really want to spend much time with each other anymore, our episodes were torture. Knowing we were always being watched by an unseen audience made an embarrassing situation even more awkward. I couldn't even stand still without wondering whether I was holding my arms dumb or worrying about whether I was blinking too much. We knew that a gray, foggy smear of invisible vuvv was everywhere around us, watching, peering at us, checking our eyes for a hint of boredom or anger or failed desire.

Once when we were pretending to kiss – our mouths stuck together uncomfortably like fried onion rings – just pressed against each other, not moving, trying not to breathe each other's breath – suddenly a word popped into my head: intimacy. The opposite of *intimate* is usually *public*. But our intimacy had been public, and so our slow failure was going to be public, too.

We wanted to just quit, but pretending we were in love was our families' only income. There was no way out. Every day we hooked up our leads and strapped English/vuvv translators onto our chests and played at hubba-hubba.

"I couldn't *wait* to see you during school!"

"Oh, Chloe! Gee willikers, the moments we spent apart were like torture."

"Really, hon?"

"Yeah. The strappado."

"I guess you think I know what that means."

"Pulling someone up by their arms behind their back so their bones break."

"Ha-ha! I'm really pleased the guy I'm going out with knows that."

"For some reason, cream puff, I've been thinking a lot about torture recently."

All of this was said with bright smiles. Forty-six vuvv subscribers were watching us. The translation boxes on our chests repeated our words out loud in the language of the vuvv.

So as we talked cutely together and batted our eyelashes at each other, all our sweet nothings were accompanied by a constant tearing and grinding.

A Georgia Peach Orchard, with the Slogan "Everything's *Peachy* in Georgia!"

The sun is big in the cartoon-blue sky above the trees. It is a postcard, the second communication from my father in the year and a half since he ran away.

"'Don't worry about me – I'm safe,'" my mom reads, and adds, "Sure, Gabe, I was gnawing my fingernails down to the bone. 'Why don't you try to rent out part of the house? You might be able to make some money that way.'" She slams the window up and yells out on to the street, as if my father were standing there, "We already did that, jackass!"

"Mom," says Nattie.

"That's it. That's all he says." My mother tosses the postcard in the air. It twiddles along for a minute through the air and lands on the brown ottoman, which enrages my mother because it didn't fall fast enough or land hard enough. She pounces on it and starts tearing it up in front of us. When she's done, she says, "I know exactly what he's doing right now."

"Right at this moment?" Nattie asks.

"He's lying to himself. That's how he's spending his afternoons. He's telling himself that he has a scheme, and he's going to make all sorts of money and send some home and be a big hero. That's his idea. He's telling himself that he isn't a bad person. 'They're better off without me,' says the salesman of the fucking year." She flings the remains of the Georgia peach orchard toward the trash. It travels in a spray.

I'm surprised. My mother is usually a very positive person, very optimistic.

I try a little optimism. I say, "At least he wrote."

"A postcard. Sure. A goddamn postcard."

"Georgia. I guess he went where it's warmer. They have a year-round growing season, and the cost of heating down there must—"

"No. He always had a weird fetish thing about southern women."

"Really?" gasps Nattie.

"Who doesn't, Mom?" I point out. "They have that accent."

"I mean he has some fantasy they're all belly-button crop tops and low-rider Daisy Dukes. It's moronic. He's going to learn soon enough that all that eye shadow smudges like hell."

Nattie walks over to the trash can and stares straight down into it, at the torn fragments, sadly. "I just can't believe his first note to us in a year is on a pun postcard."

I agree. "That's truly the unkindest cut of all."

My mom shakes her head, her mouth locked in fury.

"It's the pits," says Nattie. She waits, and we wonder why she's waiting. She explains, "That's a peach pun. The pits."

My mother lets out a long sigh. "Jesus, Nattie. I don't even know what to say to that."

My mother goes off to hunt online for jobs, she says, but I find her half an hour later doing nothing, with a screen floating in front of her, motionless. She's not looking at it, but through it, at the hazy living room on the other side. She obviously hasn't moved for a long time.

"I can't look for work again today," she says to me. "There's not going to be anything."

So we watch the news, and there has been a race riot in Central Falls. Security cameras show a bunch of white guys rampaging through a bodega, lifting up the Coke fridge and tipping it through the window, attacking the owner and his family with a baseball bat, screaming shit like go back to Mexico and leave us our jobs. They're stomping on the chips in the snack food aisle and showing their teeth like an animal pack. Some white woman standing outside on the street in a terry-cloth hoodie tells a reporter that if it weren't for those goddamn people, the censored censored censored illegals, everybody wouldn't be eating the grass in our yards on all fours.

On another channel, the pundits talk about how lazy humans are, and how if they'd just go out there and get jobs, they'd be much happier. Somewhere in the Midwest, there has been a terrorist strike against a vuvv agricultural transport – human farmers, ruined, desperate, getting revenge by detonating a fertilizer bomb in the back of a ship unloading romaine lettuces from space. "Only goddamn thing left for me to do with my fertilizer," says an industrial ag farmhand as he is led away.

And the pundits talk about how if we spent less time complaining about the vuvv and more time following their example, investing smartly in vuvv tech – if we'd just get up off our duffs, stand up from our Barcaloungers, and go out and actually work – then maybe we wouldn't all be starving and demanding food we haven't actually worked for.

I look down as he talks. I realize I actually am sitting in a Barcalounger, sunken deep in its cushions. My mother has wandered off without saying a word. She is standing in the dark of the kitchen, head bowed. The microwave blinks the wrong time.

A Village on a Mountain Peak, Taken from Some Old Master

A walled village on a mountain peak. I don't want the mountain to be barren, because I can't face rock right now. Too pitiless. I cover the mountain with pines. It will be cool under their branches in summer, and in winter they'll glow white with snow. My painting is of sometime in July, when the pine needles on the forest floor will smell sweet and hot. I add a mountain stream for bathing.

The village itself has courtyards and public squares. We'll have festivals with our friends and neighbors. We can grow things there. There's a well that gives sweet, fresh water – clean, no fucking Merrick's Disease. We won't need anything outside the village. The walls are secure on the crags. It's in a world where our enemies can't fly.

"It's nice," says Mr. Reilly, "but I like these other ones

more. The ones of your house. This one of the vuvv rendering sails. Right now, it's important to show the world as it is. It's changing so fast." He must be able to tell I'm disappointed. "Sorry, Adam," he says. "Work on whatever you want."

I nod.

"Hey," he says. "I have some good news. Really. I, um, I took the liberty of entering you in a contest. It's run by some vuvv who love human art. They want to keep the arts alive in a, you know, younger generation. That's you. They asked art teachers around the country to send in their best students' work." He smiles. "I sent in yours. A couple of photos of your paintings. Adam, I think you really have a chance at winning this thing."

"Are you kidding?" I say. I am thrilled.

"Of course I'm not kidding. You know I love your stuff. So if you pass the first round, they'll ask for more of your work. Hey, wait, wait. Best part? If you win, there's a prize. Your paintings will be reproduced and sold, you know, all over. I mean, all over the different planets. To the races we haven't even met yet. I mean, who knows if they see color like we do and all, but still, Adam, this could mean you'd sell hundreds of millions of copies. They're choosing a bunch of artists of different ages from different countries – and you would be one of the young people to represent humans across the whole Vuvv Interspecies Co-Prosperity Alliance."

"Oh – thank you!" I say. "Thank you!"

"Sure," says Mr. Reilly. "I have my fingers crossed. But I got to tell you, landscape is a hard sell with the vuvv. They think we paint still lifes. Fruit in a bowl and stuff."

"We do paint still lifes."

"They think that's all we paint. You know, they get kind of stuck on a thing. Like how they think 'traditional' human music is 1950s rock and roll. Doo-wop rock is the first thing they heard when they got here, so they think that's what we always did. Somehow they got it into their heads that still lifes are what we paint. I think it's because they can understand eating stuff. They like to think we're painting what we eat."

"I don't want to paint still lifes. I don't like still lifes. I hate painting plums. Plums are dumb."

"Still life isn't easy."

"I know. We did it in sophomore year. I did some sneakers. Everybody did some sneakers. No one could master the laces."

"I'm just warning you."

"Oh." I think about it. "Do you think I should change to still life to make the vuvv happy?"

He looks uncertain. "I don't know. I mean, maybe just the opposite. That's why I'm putting my money on you. Everybody is going to be trying to make the vuvv happy. If you just do what they're asking for, you'll never get noticed. You'll look like everyone else. I'm imagining something bolder." He flips through some of my drawings. "Look at these landscapes you've done in the last couple of years," he says. "They show what it's really like, now that the vuvv are here. They show how the Earth has changed. This is what will make you stick out. Be yourself. Tell our story. Tell the truth. That's what wins, in art: the truth."

He smiles at me. "You're going to be a better artist than I ever will be," he admits. "You're not going to have to paint castles and walled towns you want to run away to. Who knows, maybe you'll even win. Maybe they'll even take you on tour, show you off. You could see other worlds. Be ready to lose, just in case – but paint like hell, and just think what it would be like to win."

I am tingling from the praise. And late that night, the sentence that stays with me is this: "You're going to be a better artist than I ever will be." Like he's the launching pad.

I have my imaginary visions of my success someday as a painter: a Manhattan gallery engulfed by my Gothic architecture – the opening of my newest show – arches and columns and turrets floating around wealthy patrons with their hair molded in cones or stars, women in chic sheaths carrying their dogs – no, their pocket pigs – in purses, and I'm sauntering around in a holographic shirt, eating alien flora panko-fried and saying, "Tad! Tad, I think you'll particularly like this grotto. Duck through here." And I'll be super wealthy from the sale of my art, and I'll have kind of a crush on the part-time model in silver sheepskin who's trailing after me with the platter of devil-crab somethings on something, but I know I actually have a shot at a late dinner with her after the show, because I'm Adam Costello, *the* Adam Costello.

We all have our visions of crazy success.

Mr. Reilly must have had his once, too. A kid my age named Dave Reilly. He went to art school. Maybe he still secretly nurses those private visions where he's discovered and suddenly he's the big shit. I don't know.

And now he's thrown everything – all his talent, all his energy – into helping us paint and draw and sculpt and grow up. Boys who are hiding secrets, girls who can barely stand to see daylight – he has devoted his life to listening to us and giving us a space to make our statements.

That, I guess, is why he is one of the few actual *adults* I know, as opposed to people who are just old.

AUTUMN IN A FIELD NEAR A DISCHARGE FACILITY

Mr. Reilly tells me that I need to practice painting the atmosphere of Earth itself. He shows me the paintings of the Hudson River School, the great American landscape artists of the nineteenth century, who created a world of peaks and chasms, quiet lakes, tiny figures teetering on the edge of waterfalls. These images hang all around him in the air as he calls them up for me. "Ironically, they were painted for the great industrialists," he says, "to show the beauty of the landscape they were ruining."

He is anxious because it is almost time for him to go to his doorman job up in the sky. "Think about air," he says. "When I look out of the windows in that apartment building, what do I see?"

"The ground?" I guess. "And rich people?"

"No. I see the atmosphere. That's what these Hudson River School painters saw, too. The atmosphere. Clouds. Mist. Moisture. Look at these paintings. They're not paintings of things. Mountains or trees. They're paintings of the air between things. The only reason they paint actual things at all – like stumps and hills or the sea – is so you can judge what the air's like in front of them. It was, you know, a big deal for the Hudson River painters to get the light right as it fell through the air. Think about the gulfs in between the mountains and the forests. You should be able to tell if it's about to rain, or if it hasn't rained in weeks. You should be able to feel the air on your face." He tells me, "In a good landscape painting, you should be able to guess the barometric pressure."

Chloe and I go to a field near a big, bulbous discharge facility, and I try painting the landscape in fall. I am concentrating on the way the light suggests air. The leaves are all burnt orange. A lot of them are tangled in the tall grass. The milkweed pods have exploded; they're drooling foam into the bracken.

My stomach is giving me a lot of problems. I am glad we are outside – it lets the smell drift away on the wind – but I'm worried I might have sudden diarrhea.

Chloe obviously doesn't want to be there, watching me paint. A few months earlier, my art seemed romantic to her. Now she is just impatient. She wants to go hang out with her friends, instead of with a loser like me.

She doesn't say "a loser like you," because we are on the clock. She doesn't have to say it, though. I can read it in her eyes and a furious part of her upper lip.

"Adam? It's great just being here with you, sitting in the cold near a discharge facility, but do you think we could go over to Courtney's house? Hmm, Ads?"

"It's just that I'm trying to paint for this important art contest, and the field is out here. They don't keep it at Courtney's."

"You aren't actually painting. You're standing, holding your brush."

"I have to wait for the sun to come out from behind the cloud. See? It'll really kindle those trees." I'm starting to feel impatient. I want to scream that I wish she'd go the hell away and leave me to paint in peace. I squint up at the sky. "It'll just be another fifteen or twenty minutes."

"But doesn't my smile light up those trees? Like the sun coming out from behind a cloud?"

"Sure, my poppet."

"Great, sweetums. So start slopping the paint on your board."

"See, Mr. Reilly wants me to paint the space between things. That's what's important. The Hudson River School used color to mark the atmosphere."

73

"Oh, today you're sure as hell marking the atmosphere," she snaps.

"Are you talking about my disease? Which I can't help?"

She's about to scream at me. I can tell. I warn her with my eyes. Our families are depending on us. She turns away and walks off to balance on a white log.

I crane my neck up at the clouds. The sun is about to come out any minute, and then I'll get the right colors.

I look back at Chloe, facing away from me on the log. Something about seeing her there alone on that log, in that field, with her tennis shoes in a plié, makes me remember why I liked her a few months ago.

"Chloe, honey," I say. Something in my voice tells her I am real. She turns and actually smiles.

"Let's not fight," she says, swallowing something.

The cloud is sliding away from the sun. I dip my brush and prepare to paint.

"Here comes the sun," I say.

Then a rich-person house drifts over and stops. We are totally in shadow.

It's a good thing we laughed and made up. The vuvv who watch love the reconciliation. It is one of our most popular episodes ever.

HUMAN IDOL EMPORIUM
(Buddy Gui's House)

My gouache painting of Buddy Gui's house – about a mile away from our house – shows his garage door open and all his chain-saw sculptures dragged out onto his driveway.

I don't know Buddy Gui well. He's also a senior; he plays baseball. That's about all I know.

This is how I first take real notice of him.

Chloe and I are walking arm in arm past a food line. Other people are waiting for handouts. We've just bought our families stuff at the vuvvmart. Our vuvv hookups are turned on, so we're mooning like lovers, but lovers who secretly hate each other.

"The only way you could be any cuter, love-bucket," says Chloe to me, "is if I drilled dimples in your cheeks." She laughs sweetly. "With an awl, pumpkin. A really sharp one."

"You know the best thing about all this food?" I say, smiling like torture. "We know we'll be eating it together."

Chloe tries to come up with a reply that isn't tearing all the hair off my head.

So I say, "Maybe we could share the same spoon."

Suddenly she grabs my shirt.

"Surprise kiss?" I pucker obnoxiously.

"No. This way." She pulls us into an alley.

"What's wrong?" I ask, though I can tell what's wrong: the gaggle of rich kids from Mr. Reilly's hovering apartment building are heading our way. She doesn't want to be seen with me when we're holding plastic grocery bags full of cheap shit.

I proclaim loudly, "Wuv-buckle, I like to walk out in the open, where the sunlight streams down and catches the amber highlights burned chemically into your hair." I figure this should sting.

She pushes me deeper into the alley. "Back here," she says, trying to sound brutally seductive, "we can be alone."

"Weren't those some of our dear friends, honey? Wouldn't you like us to 'hang' with them? Exchanging jokes and fancy words?"

"Alleys were made for love."

"When you've got something special like we do, how can you hide it under a bushel? How can you snuff it under a snuffer? Why, Chlo-Chlo, I want to shout it to the wondering world!" I open my mouth wide enough to show my tonsils flapping, and when I can tell she is about to pick up a piece of rebar and knock off my block, I bellow, *"I love you, Chl—"*

She kisses me fiercely. Awfully, I feel her tongue trying to wiggle its ghastly way into my mouth cavity. My stomach lurches. Our vuvv speaking-horns clack together on our chests. I can't believe a few months ago I wanted to grope the breasts skewed between the straps of her translator. We are nothing special anymore. Whatever possessed us, when we were in love, has departed. We are just animals. She has udders; I have acne. There is no romance. My stomach lurches again.

I swear and push her away. Diarrhea.

I clutch but can't hold. I feel it spilling down the backs of my legs. I stagger against the wall.

She can tell what is happening. I can't stand her look of disgust.

For a minute we face each other. Then she starts tearing off the hookups to her senses. She pulls them off her head, one by one.

"Can't take it," she says, and it isn't to me. She picks up her translator and yells into it, "I can't take it! It's over!" The translator scratches the message out in vuvv.

Invisibly, a cloud of viewers swirls around us, watching every move.

77

"Chloe!" I plead. She is throwing away two families' incomes. "Come on!"

Cramps hit. I gasp and grab at my stomach. Shitting it all out would actually feel good – like the disease itself would leave with the watery crap, and for a second, I'd be free of it, because there it would all be, drying on my calves.

"I'm seeing someone else," says Chloe. "Buddy Gui."

"Buddy Gui?" I protest.

"Buddy was following our site, and he could tell we were having trouble. He sent me a comment."

"Oh, I'll send you a comment."

"What does that mean?"

"Buddy Gui is a total meathead. I'm an artist. I'm going to have my work entered in an interplanetary contest."

"Well, as it happens, he's an artist too."

"Oh, is he?"

"He makes chain-saw sculptures."

"Is that an artist?"

"Sorry. Is someone who craps down the back of their legs an artist?"

"Fair point."

"Expressing yourself?"

The kids from the floating building have heard her yelling. They have turned the corner and are staring at us. At me, really.

"I suffer," I tell them, somewhat ridiculously, "from a

syndrome known as Merrick's Disease. I'm saving for a vuvv treatment."

I move my legs slowly, like a lizard, like a Komodo dragon, because all the inside folds of my pants are filled with hot crap and I do not want to feel the wet on my socks.

Chloe walks away.

"See you at home, dear!" I call sadly, for the benefit of my vuvv hookup.

She tells me to go do something to myself that we used to do together.

It is over. My relationship, my job, my income for the family. I squelch home. It is drizzling down the heels of my shoes and is getting clammy.

I sit in the bathroom for hours after showering. I run my clothes under the tub's faucet. I have to wash them in the machine, but for that, I'd have to go downstairs and pass by the rooms where Chloe's family lives. I can't face them.

The next day, I walk by Buddy Gui's house. I really don't know him, except by sight, and do not go there out of jealousy. Chloe and Gui can stay together forever, embracing in a paper heart while songbirds tweedle the flippin' dee-dee. I just want to check out Gui as an artist.

It appears that Gui is trying to sell his chain-saw sculptures to alien tourists. Up on his roof, he has painted a bunch of scratches that are vuvv. The message must say something about souvenirs for sale.

Buddy is hacking into a stump with his chain saw. I admire the way he controls his wrists. He truly is an artist. I am surprised, however, at what he is carving: fat Buddhas hanging on the Christian Cross.

"Hello," I say. "I can't help but notice that you're carving a fat crucified Buddha."

"Yup." He puts down his chain saw.

That seems to me like a good start.

"Is it a statement?" I say. "A hard-hitting indictment of society's blindness?"

"No. It's a souvenir for the vuvv. They love human religion. They think we're really spiritual. I saw some of them selling these Buddha crucifixes to other vuvv tourists. They hang them on their walls and say it's the god of the humans. It makes them feel good."

"Because we're primitive."

"Yeah." He points at my chest to show me I've got it. "Primitive. They think we get them in touch with something old or simple. And I thought: Okay, if I, a real live human being person, carve these things myself, by hand, huge, those vuvv are going to go apeshit."

"Oh? By hand? Is that what you're doing?"

"Yeah. The chain saw is in my hand." He picks it up and waggles it in my face.

"Agreed."

"I'm telling you. They're going to go freakin' apeshit."

His yard is full of the crucified Buddhas. I ask smartly, "So. Sold many already? You had a run on them yet?" The unsold statues recede back into the darkness of the garage, pudgy arms held out in supplication.

He looks at me kind of cockeyed. "You Adam Costello?"

"Fellow artist."

"Poopy-pants Costello?"

"I suppose it—"

"Ass-blast Costello?"

"No one ever understands performance art when it's on the cutting edge."

He gestures to his chain saw. "I'll show you the cutting edge, you don't get your leaky ass out of here."

"I gather you're going out with Chloe Marsh," I say breezily. "I know her because her family rents from our family."

"Downwind of you?"

"Mr. Gui, I believe that's unkind."

"Don't call me Mr. G— What the hell you here for?"

"A fellow artist. I'm actually up for an international, interplanetary art award."

"Just don't, you know, Jackson Pollock all over the grass."

"Oh, har-dee-har-har. You're selling out the human race.

81

You're a traitor to our history." I look around. "Or you would be, if you had any customers."

"Let me repeat that I do my best work with a chain saw."

He hefts it and gives a couple pulls on the trigger. The motor revs. "Love to chat," I say, "but I need to catch the late afternoon light on some birches across town."

Then I leave.

When I get home, I pace around in circles in my room. Finally I start to paint. I paint Buddy Gui's house and his stupid Buddhas. I paint the dark, miserable sky and the plastic bagging his parents have stapled over their windows. I want his display of chain-saw art and his sign for the aliens overhead to all look as stupid and pathetic as they possibly can. I slash at the canvas with my fingers spludged in gray. I wipe off my hand and pick up my brush again.

But as I paint Buddy Gui with his chain saw, standing in the wood chips, buzzing away at another pine Buddha, I start to slow down. I want to really get that movement of his elbows and wrists, the way he knew how to wield a chain saw. People are hard. They move around a lot, and it's difficult when you're not doing VR, but on a canvas, to show what motion might be like when nothing can move.

Staring at that figure I painted, I realize there is something sad about the chain-saw artistry of Buddy Gui. Here we all are, struggling to be noticed, trying to be what the vuvv want us to be. We all have to find some way to live with the world as it is now. We all have to become something new, something the vuvv want, each one of us trying to translate the thoughts of the vuvv from something that just sounds to us like scratching and broken zippers.

As it turns out, my landscape of Gui's Human Idol Emporium is not sarcastic at all, I don't think. Instead, it looks like a human trying to hew a life and a belief out of nothing but dead wood – which is, in its own way, heroic.

A LOCAL VUVV COMPOUND

The vuvv compound rises out of suburbia, a collection of towers, buttresses, and bulbs of green metal. All the houses in the neighborhood used to be expensive, but now they're all covered with a layer of black soot. The trees there are dead, even in the summertime. In winter, the snow is gray. Smoke pours out of holes in the vuvv compound.

Chloe and I have to report there to talk about our love and its problems. We announce ourselves in the foyer, and we're led into some kind of a thing, which goes up with us to an office. A vuvv is there, with symbols hanging around it in the air. It's spreading some kind of sauce on itself.

It scratches out some *hellos*. Our earbuds translate. The vuvv don't wear translators – they say it's up to us to speak their language, if we want to do business with them. They can't be expected to learn the languages of all the different species they deal with, babbling across the galaxy, some of them speaking in smells or patterned light.

"What's the problem?" I say. "We are really still in love."

Chloe sighs dramatically. I hate her again. If we can't save this relationship, our families will starve.

"You are not in love," says the vuvv. "Our clients can tell."

I reach out to squeeze Chloe's hand. "We are abso-*cute*-ly in love. Swack, swack!"

She lashes out and knuckles my fingers hard.

I shake my hand to deaden the pain. I explain, "Lovers' tiff."

"Your pupils don't dilate as they once did," the vuvv complains.

"Don't cut off our channel," I plead. "Part of love is loss. The vuvv should understand that!"

"That was not our agreement."

"Human life isn't all posies and roses. We'll bring you drama!"

"Human love is forever," the vuvv informs us. "It lasts until the end of time."

Suddenly, Chloe lunges in to speak. "So I'll do another channel," she says. "With this guy Buddy Gui. We're the real thing." (Traitor.)

The vuvv responds, "I repeat that human love lasts until the end of time. If it does not, it is not love."

"Sure," says Chloe. "Of course. Adam and me wasn't real love. If you want to see—"

"But you offered love," says the vuvv. "It was the product you were selling. And what you produced was not love. It was fake love. You defrauded us. It's clear. Your heart rates no longer rise when you see each other."

"Well," says Chloe, "they do when I want to slug him."

"Our guests demand genuine tachycardia. And *you*," it says, meaning me, "though your secretions are ample, we suspect they don't arise from excitation. And they seem unlovely to your partner. I am saying, both of you are guilty of fraud."

My stomach is sinking.

"You have a choice," says the vuvv. "You can prove your love is eternal; or you can admit it is not, and you can return all your year's income from this fraudulent venture; or we can have our lawyers sue you for misrepresentation."

I splutter about the income. It is over a thousand dollars each now, and we've spent it each month just to get our families food.

"Stop making bursts of sound," says the vuvv. "I am a specialist in human affection and its monetization. You've heard me: either display true love forever – impossible, as your constricted pupils and nonplussed micro-gestures demonstrate – or you give back the money our guests spent on you."

Chloe and I stare in horror. There is no way we can pretend; but there is no way we could give the money back, even if we wanted to. And a vuvv lawsuit will ruin us – vuvv law costs people more than they will earn in twelve lifetimes.

"Perhaps a romantic poem I wrote 'in the human style' will help you understand," says the vuvv. Chloe and I are speechless. The vuvv begins:

> Now, my darling, comes the glorious spring,
> And I find true beauty in your everything:
> Your arms, so slender, and your meaty shanks,
> Your long head-bristles that hang down in hanks;
> The discolored skin around the hole with which you bite,
> The wet face-patches, so sensitive to light …

My stomach is in rebellion. The blood has left my face. I stop listening to the voice rolling along in my earbud. Without the translation, the vuvv's ode, its scratchy iambs and dactyls, sound like someone walking forcefully in corduroys. We are going to starve to death because of this idiot. My family is going to have our house taken away. The vuvv don't care if you can't pay. They take everything you have.

I walk out of the office without even saying good-bye. I feel sick. Behind me, I hear Chloe interrupting and saying, "Please, please – this guy Buddy…"

I come home and I do my homework. There is nothing else to do. Nothing matters, but I keep on doing the homework. I sketch the vuvv compound. All the tiny houses at its feet are coated in black. I scratch the black darker, and darker, and more violent, until there's nothing but a haze of scribbles, and their fortress sits in a lake of shadow.

My House in December

There are no Christmas ornaments up. The vuvv like us to have Christmas – they find its weird traditions charming, and they're deeply moved by its effect on consumer expenditure – but we don't have the money to spend on extra electricity for lights, and, plus, I feel very private about our suitcases of ornaments, hidden away since Dad ran off. I don't want them to be out where Chloe and the other Marshes can see them.

We eat oatmeal for the first week after Chloe and I are fired. We've got to make our money last.

Mom says, "We could sell the car."

Nattie points out, "You'll need it when you get a job."

"Well, if worse comes to worst, though. It hardly has any miles on it."

So we spoon out the oatmeal, and we somehow get by.

Unbelievably, Chloe is angry at me, as if I'm the one who messed things up. She is hanging out with Buddy Gui, artist, all the time.

Chloe's brother, Hunter, is paid a little for working part-time at the rendering plant, but the Marshes have told us they're not giving us any of his wages in rent. They know it will take us months to get them evicted. They eat delicacies like Slim Jims in front of us while we spoon down our oatmeal. My mother and Mr. Marsh yell about it all the time. They are both home all day, so they have nothing to do but yell.

Meanwhile, Hunter Marsh has started to really drive me crazy through the floor. He is trying to learn vuvv. I hear him in the basement, expectorating back to a vuvv language soundtrack. *KcckckKHKHTvrchik. At what time does the saucer leave for Denver? KcckckKHKHTvrchik... Ffffrkkhh. You appear fertile, as if you could bud many spawn. This is a traditional vuvv greeting. Ffffrkkhh.*

He worships the vuvv playboys he works for. He talks about them all the time and wants to be just like them, with their cool apartments in the upper air and their devices for hovering. One day when I go downstairs to flip the circuit breaker, I catch Hunter on all fours, trying to walk like a vuvv, with his back to the floor.

The Parking Lot
of the Looted
Old Stop & Shop

The huge plate-glass windows of the Stop & Shop have been broken for a couple of years, since people looted the store during a hunger riot. Stop & Shop never bothered to reopen the branch. The racks are all there in the shadows, but everything is covered with graffiti. The other stores in the strip mall are empty. I paint it early in the morning, when the ice in the parking lot is an electric blue, and in the sky up above, the rendering sails burn red. The shadows are stark and sharp. I try to catch some of the gleams on broken glass. It's hard, since the shards are tiny and far away.

When I tell Mr. Reilly about it in the hall, he says to me that it sounds great, and I should meet him with my full portfolio after school. He has a surprise for me. I can barely wait.

The school day seems to stretch forever, especially

because my last couple of classes are taught by vuvv tech, which just shows us stuff floating in the air and then tells us off when we act like jerks.

When I go into the art room, Mr. Reilly looks very nervous. He kind of babbles hello. I can't tell what his problem is, until I walk around the table and see a vuvv down near his knees.

"This is Shirley," says Mr. Reilly. "It loves, you know, human art."

I gape at the vuvv. I try to think of something to say. I suspect it's important to turn on the charm. "You appear fertile, as if you could bud many spawn."

Shirley is clearly flattered. It announces, "Six already!" Its squat body is dangling with paddles that smell of each of its young. We can't really smell the difference, but it's a matter of pride to vuvv. Shirley rattles its paddles.

"I've seen some of your work," says Shirley. "I am just so impressed that you use actual paint."

I try to smile at it. I don't know whether it will recognize a smile. Some of them know what facial expressions mean; some of them don't.

"I just love the human race. You people are so much more spiritual than we are. We've lost the path, you know, with all this commercialization." It makes a motion with some of its stumps that must mean something. "This is why we're so excited about this contest, Adam Costello. Some of the beautiful work of the human young will be exported to the stars."

It waits for me to say something. "Uh, thank you," I say. "I'm really excited too."

"You've already passed the first round. That is wonderful. I'm here to pick up your latest work. Over the next few weeks, the jury will be judging the work of about a thousand teenage American artists. Two lucky spawn from each state of the American union will be chosen to be sent to a gala art exhibition in March."

"Oh, wow."

"The gala will happen in orbit. It is a fancy affair. And that night we'll announce the all-American teen spawn artist winner."

"Great."

"It is." The vuvv reaches up with a limb and flips through images of my paintings of castles, mountains, and walled towns. "Now, Adam, tell me: Why landscapes, when traditionally humans paint fruit?"

I say vague things about how we humans painted landscapes sometimes, too, and that I'm painting the world I want to live in: a world of adventure but also of ancient beauty. Something like that.

"But they're not real places," Shirley confirms.

"No," I admit. "But I do have these, which are of real

places around town here." I call up images of my other paintings. Mr. Reilly nods to me and crosses his fingers.

Shirley looks through my paintings of the rendering sails, the discharge facility, Heather's Bucket of Broth, my house in all seasons.

It asks, "But why so sad? Don't you want to give a positive image of your world to the rest of the universe? Do you really think that this is what other species want to see when they look at the work of a young human artist? They don't want to see vuvv tech. Members of the Vuvv Interspecies Co-Prosperity Alliance can see that anywhere, on any planet. But they want the Earth as it was before we came. They want to see what makes the Earth special." It waits for me to answer.

When I don't say anything, it turns back to the fantasy paintings. "These are much more beautiful," Shirley says. "They give a sense of the Earth's history. Your fortifications. I particularly admire the paradoxical way they capture the ruggedness of your world's barbarian age with consummate elegance. They show the peculiarity of the human imagination. Allow me to take these as your entries."

Now that Shirley has said this – even though it is praising my work – I don't exactly feel proud. I have to admit, I wish it liked the real ones more. Those are the ones I want it to take.

Shirley insists, "No one on another world is going to want a picture of a vuvv discharge facility hanging on the wall of their gorging chamber or their dormancy pit. They want to see beautiful, strange vistas of an exotic world far away, where they might vacation for a period of days to weeks, depending on their work availability and gravitational jump-space time displacement."

I feel choked. I want to tell it to take the others, to taste and swallow the truth.

Mr. Reilly says, "It's your decision, Adam."

My family needs the money. It would change our lives forever. But when I glance at my fantasy paintings, they no longer look like any place I want to be. Or they are what I want, but I am already here in this world, wrapped up in the blighted towns and the peeling paint and the glow of the rendering sails at night and in the looted Stop & Shop at first light. That is where I really am. That is where my family is stuck. And that's what I have to deal with. Without flinching.

So that's it. My decision is made.

"Okay," I say meekly. "Take the castles and the walled towns."

Shirley is clearly pleased. "Excellent," it says. "I think with these images you have a very good shot at winning, Adam Costello. David Reilly, you collect the actual, physical canvases to be delivered and you submit them to the jury. Adam Costello, you will hear in a month about this second round. With luck, I will see you next in orbit, at the grand gala opening – where the final winner will be announced!"

"Thank you," I say, gloomily, as if I've just signed up for hard labor.

I say good-bye to them both, mumbling, and back out of the room. Mr. Reilly calls out that I should drop the paintings by his doorman job. He can mail them from there; the mail is faster from aerial housing. The jitney, which is what rich people call the shuttle, goes up at seven, and I can drop the pieces off then.

I walk home on the cracked sidewalks, thinking about what I've done. I open the front door and there, of course, is Chloe, heading downstairs to her bedroom with Buddy Gui. They stare at me and don't even say hello. Once they disappear, I hear the ruckus from some buddy-cop holoshow they're watching, or else they've just turned the volume up real loud to hide the sound of them fucking.

I throw myself down on the sofa. There's nothing I feel like doing. The talking from the show vibrates the floor. "I don't just say, 'No.' I say, 'HELL NO.' I say, 'HELLUVA NO, FARM BOY!'"

The thought of her in Gui's arms makes my stomach twist up, and I can't stand it.

A little later, Nattie gets home and walks through the door, half-singing pop favorites by clicking her tongue musically against the roof of her mouth. Mom comes in right behind her.

Mom says, "Hey, honey. How was your day?"

I shrug part of a shoulder. She tells me about hers. She applied for a cashier job at a convenience store. "Lot of other applicants," she says. "Maybe a thirty/seventy percent chance. It's not about me or my qualifications. I worked at a bank. I can transition into a job like that no trouble. It's just a question of how many people are applying."

Nattie keeps clicking a song with her tongue, now bouncing on and off the hassock on her knees. She lands on her feet, arms outspread, and reports, "The Marshes have the holo up too loud. It sounds like I have cops in my head."

"I got some good news," I say, feeling as if I've already lost. "I made it to the next round of that art contest."

Nattie and my mom are overjoyed. They make a big fuss over it.

Then Nattie says, "I have some good news, too! I have a boyfriend. His name is Michael. We're going to do what you did."

I'm confused. "Date someone who thinks you're pathetic and then leaves you for a guy who makes art with a chain saw?"

"No!" says Nattie. "We're going to sign up to 1950s-date for the vuvv."

I push myself to my feet. "No way! No! No, no, no, Nattie! No. You're not doing it."

"Michael's totally into it. We'll learn all the old 1950s terms, like you did."

"You're twelve. Twelve. You saw what happened to Chloe and me. We're screwed. And it was sick."

"We need money for the family!"

"No!"

"No," agrees my mother. "We'll sell the car or the house before I'll have you do that. It was a big mistake for Adam—"

"Thanks."

"And it would be even worse for you."

"I want to do something!" Nattie insists. "All we ever do is complain and eat ramen! Mom, you said we should be proactive."

"Not what I'm talking about. Not."

"All right," says Nattie. "I'll tell Michael, 'Sorry, dream-boat.'"

"Good," says my mother.

But that's not enough for me. "You're scheming, aren't you? You're thinking you're going to do it in secret. I can tell."

Nattie looks sheepish.

I continue, wagging my finger, "You think you're going to do this and then you'll bring home surprise money and we'll buy food and all have a party, and you, Cindy Lou Who, will carve the roast beast. Well, no. No, Nattie."

She still looks too sly for my taste.

I say, "I'll tie you to the towel rack for the next two weeks if I have to. We'll bring you oatmeal and homework."

"Listen to your brother," says Mom. "I love you like my own leg, but that's an incredibly stupid idea."

And heartbreaking, I think to myself later, as I'm flipping through my paintings. Why do things have to be like this?

I collect a folder of sketches and a stack of five paintings and box them up. I wrap some packing tape around them to close the package and to make a handle. Then I head down to the shuttle pad for workers who have to be taken up to the hovering homes.

The jitney takes about twenty minutes to drop me off at Mr. Reilly's work. The whole time, I'm thinking about what my mom and Nattie and I are going to do, and I'm panicking that Nattie would even think of doing the vuvv 1950s hookup. It's awful. Strangely, I feel shame at our family. It's not our fault we don't have jobs and don't have money, I know, but, still, I feel embarrassed.

I go through the service entrance, lugging my box of paintings. Mr. Reilly looks tired when I see him. He's sagging a bit in his uniform, slumped behind his counter.

"Hey, Mr. Reilly. How are things?"

He rolls his head. "Long day. It's tough to go straight from teaching to this."

"Yeah," I say. "I bet. So, I brought—"

One of the foyer doors slides open and in walk a couple of the kids who'd admired my castle last time – a boy and a girl, giggling and leaning on each other. I can't remember if either of these two were with the crowd who saw Chloe breaking up with me on that horrible day. The boy's wearing some kind of ultra-preppy casual space suit with the letters IEVA on it, weathered to look like it has been knocked around in meteor storms and baked by the radiation of a thousand suns, when actually he just bought a goddamn jumpsuit online.

I realize I'm standing behind the desk, which makes it appear I'm a friend of Mr. Reilly's, instead of a rich kid visiting his aunt in the building. Moment of panic, then, about being caught out in our earlier lie – then I'm lashed with guilt, because of course I *am* a friend of Mr. Reilly's.

Mr. Reilly says, "Good evening, Connor, Juniper."

"Hey, Dave," says the boy. Then he notices me. "You're that kid with the little magic castle." He and the girl exchange a glance, smirking. "With your girlfriend. We saw you in that alley."

I nod, rocking backward, recalling the disaster.

"You have lots of bathrooms in your magic castle? You know, for if you're playing house and you need to take a virtual crap?"

"Now, Connor," says Mr. Reilly. "I don't think that's —"

"See you, Dave," says the boy, and he and his girlfriend

100

saunter off to the elevators together.

When they're gone, Mr. Reilly uncomfortably says, "I'm sorry about that, Adam. I don't know exactly what they were, ah..." He just waves his hand without finishing the sentence.

"Yeah," I say, and we stand in awkward silence. Outside the big windows, a freezing rain is falling. The building is in cloud.

We start to talk about sending the paintings to the contest, and Mr. Reilly searches for the address and reads it out to me as I Magic Marker it onto the box. We're just putting clear tape over the address when the docking bay door opens again and a mom with a screaming kid comes in.

"Evening, Mrs. Gregson," says Mr. Reilly, while the little girl screams over him, "I don't want it *ever*! I won't eat it! I don't want it!" She throws a clamshell box on the ground. It pops open. It's apparently leftovers from a restaurant.

"Kennedy," the mother says, "you reach out your little hands and pick that up right now."

The kid shoves the box farther away with her foot.

"And who's this?" says Mrs. Gregson, looking at me as if wondering why I'm allowed to stand there, in her foyer, behind the doorman's desk.

"This is one of my students," Mr. Reilly explains, over the *thunk* of the little girl doing judo kicks. "One of my best students, Mrs. Gregson. His name is Adam Costello. You'll be reading about him in art journals one day soon. I don't think she should be kicking the plate-glass windows like that."

"Kennedy, cease. Stop it, Kennedy! I'd forgotten you were a teacher, Dave. I thought you were an artist."

"Oh, I do a little painting, but my real vocation is teaching promising young people like Mr. Costello here."

"Well," Mrs. Gregson says cheerily, "you know the old joke: 'Those who can, do; those who can't, teach!'" She laughs.

Mr. Reilly shrinks, and I want to jump over the desk and smack her. I'm thinking of all the students in the town six thousand feet below us who love him, who hardly ever hear a kind word, who only have him telling them that they're worth anything. I choke out, "Mr. Reilly's an amazing teacher. He changes people's lives. He buys the art supplies for the class himself."

"That's so great," says Mrs. Gregson, without interest. "I said stop kicking the windows, Kennedy. What if one fell out?"

"They're reinforced glass," says Mr. Reilly. "But those smudges might be hard to get off."

"And pick up the steak."

"It's floor steak, now, Mom," says Kennedy.

"Pick it up! If you don't want it, someone will. Pick it up! Maybe Dave would want it. Dave? It's perfectly good. We just got it at Wind Song."

Mr. Reilly looks at the box on the floor. "Well, no, that's okay, Mrs.—"

"Give it to Dave," the mother commands. "Right now. Give your leftovers to Dave."

The little girl picks up the steak and closes the clamshell box. She walks over and lays it on the desk.

"There," says Mrs. Gregson. "Now Dave can have it for dinner. To thank him for being so nice to you always." She explains, "It's most of a porterhouse steak. She only ate seven or eight bites. She said it was too gristly."

The little girl folds her arms.

The mother prompts gently, "Now, maybe Dave wants to say thank you. Maybe he wants to say thank you for being such a nice girl and giving him supper." When Mr. Reilly doesn't, Mrs. Gregson says, "Would you mind? It would help her learn an important lesson about charity and kindness." She can't understand why Mr. Reilly is hesitating. She adds, "I mean, she is giving you dinner. Thanks, Dave."

I can't stand watching this. I look at the screens floating behind the desk.

"Well, thanks, Kennedy," says Mr. Reilly, defeated. "It's very kind of you to give me your dinner."

The little girl doesn't listen but drags her mother toward the elevators.

They disappear. After the doors close, we hear the girl

taking ninja kicks at the sliding doors. The kicks ascend into the ceiling.

For a second, we don't say anything. It's like Mr. Reilly wants me to forget what just happened, and I want him to forget what just happened.

But then, appalled, I see Mr. Reilly pulling the clamshell box toward himself. "Shouldn't let it, you know, go to waste." Unable even to meet my eyes, he picks up a morsel of steak in his fingers and starts eating.

I don't want him to eat the steak of humiliation. He chews for a while. "It's not gristly," he points out. "It's incredible. Even cold. Now, about your entry—"

"No," I say. "I'm not entering these paintings. I brought the wrong ones."

He looks at me in surprise.

I drop the portfolio on the floor. "I'm not entering these pictures. Fuck castles. Fuck them! No." I kick the paintings as petulantly as the girl kicked her dinner. "I'm sending the others. The paintings and drawings of our town."

I'm overwhelmed by my decision. Even as I say it, I know it's stupid. My family is barely scraping by, and here I am taking a risk, being selfish, being an asshole artist. But somehow I'm also sure that this is right, and that this is what my mother would want me to do. "If you want something badly enough," she says, "be true to yourself, and work like hell, and

104

you can do anything." It's her can-do attitude. I am sure that Nattie and she would be behind me a hundred percent. "I'll bring up the other paintings tomorrow."

"Adam, I think you'll have a better chance of impressing the vuvv judges and winning with—"

"No," I say. "No, I'm going to say to them what everybody should be saying to them. 'This is our world. You're part of the reason our world is this way.'"

"You could be throwing this away," Mr. Reilly warns me. "Out the window." But then his face breaks into a smile. "And I'm proud of you for it."

THE DRIVEWAY, EMPTY
(Pencil on paper)

It isn't long after I submit my new work for the contest that I get a fever and it's clear my Merrick's Disease is getting worse. My mother says it's because I'm worried about money and art. Maybe that's so. I guess I developed some kind of canker sores in my intestines because of the Merrick's, and filth leaked out into the rest of my body. It's spreading infection, sepsis. I can't stop shivering. My teeth are literally clacking together. They sound like a vuvv pep rally.

I lie in my bed all day. My mom is worried about me. I need to keep drinking and drinking. My mom boils the dirty tap water to sterilize it and then puts it outside in the snow to cool it. We're doing without a fridge for the winter, since there's the weather instead.

I have the shits all the time. I struggle into the bathroom

where I sag against the wall, staring bleary-eyed at the ring of products around the sink. Chloe and Hunter use the same bathroom as me. Hunter is trying to lose all his hair to be more like his vuvv bosses. A bottle of Alopeesh-Sure ("Guaranteed Glabrous!") is tipped onto its side. Hour after hour, doubled over with cramps, I sit there reading the label stupidly, unable to think of anything except my own shivering discomfort.

My doctor says he can help my symptoms, but we don't have the coverage to do anything vuvv about the disease itself. He gives me antibiotics and hopes they'll at least kill the infection I got from the intestinal sores.

My fever gets worse, and during one terrible evening I start to hallucinate. There is a corridor that leads right through my one wall and then out the other wall. People walk through the corridor, and all of them are coming to see me. I am just in a T-shirt and underwear, so I tell them to stop. I am supposed to hide until I'm dressed. All the hallucinations come over and, one by one, inspect me. They all nod. The awful burning in my gut somehow means I am bad. They can see it. They tell each other that I am definitely bad and point to my stomach. I shout at them that it is not fair, because they should have given me time to prepare.

My mother is standing beside my bed, telling me that no one else is there. Just her. No one else.

"And me!" shouts Hunter Marsh from the room below.

"I'm not magic. I'm just sleeping. So shut up!"

My mother brings me some cold water to drink. I go back to sleep, but wake up sometime in the dark belly of night. Everything looks strange. Shadows rain down on the wall; it is snowing outside. I am so hot, I feel as if my skin is covered with a scum of red clay.

I drink the last of the water by my bed. I get up and shuffle into the dark kitchen. There is no more boiled water left. Giardia, norovirus, hepatitis, Legionnaires'. Drinking raw tap water is like wringing out roadkill onto your tongue. But my organs are all so hot. The heat is unbearable. I decide to eat snow.

I go to the front door and open it. Snow falls lazily over the neighborhood, lying in lines along the slats of the vinyl siding next door. I sit down on the front stoop and grab a handful of snow. It's delicious. I'm eating it like popcorn, gorging off my palm, when I see a figure in the dark.

It looks like my father.

"Adam," it says.

"Dad." I lower my hand from my mouth.

"Hey." Then I realize: "Oh. Right. Hallucinating."

He has entered my fever dream without dressing for snow. He's wearing a short-sleeved polo shirt, as if he's standing in a Georgia peach grove, and I've just cut and pasted him randomly into winter. For some reason, in my fever dream he's clutching a cheap chrome trophy.

He squints at me.

I say, "So I'm delirious."

"Oh. Yeah," he agrees, like he's embarrassed to be a hallucination.

We don't say anything for a minute. Just because he's a product of my imagination doesn't mean he shouldn't speak first. Even as a delusion, he's a fucking coward. The shape of him just stands there, blotted out by snow.

I try, "I miss you. The actual you."

"I miss you, too. I miss you and Nattie so much."

"Swell, Dad."

"That's why I've come here," says the specter of my father. "That's why I'm standing in front of you right now. I want to tell you and Nattie how much I miss you. And I love you."

The snow slants across his face. It glistens on the trophy in his hands.

"You're staying where it's warm," I say.

He nods.

I demand, "Why did you leave us? How could you... How could you do that?" I accuse him, "You told us you were gone on a postcard with a peach pun."

The apparition grips his trophy under an arm and turns out his palms as if to say, "I don't know," or maybe "I'm sorry." The snow catches on his arm hairs. He tries to smile.

He announces, "Georgia has just voted to change its logo from a whole peach to a peach with a bite taken out of it."

I glare at him.

He suggests, "Maybe it's supposed to make it look more ... I dunno ... delicious."

"What's the trophy for?"

He hugs it to his chest and nervously answers, "Winning."

I squint at the trophy – maybe it's for basketball, maybe it's a layup – but what it looks like is a human who's reaching with all his might for the sky, but just can barely touch the globe.

And the specter of my father speaks a message out of the darkness:

"Before I go... You'll... Will you tell your mother I'm doing what's best for you? She won't understand, but I have a plan. I know what I'm doing. I'm going to start a business. I need a little capital, and I'm going to set something up. You know I can provide for this family. Remember, tell her: I bought your mom's car for her. I got a great deal on both the cars. It's important to remember that. I bought it for her. If there's one thing I am, I'm a great salesman. Salesman of the year. Now I've got the capital, I'm going to start a business and work for myself. Rug cleaning, okay? As soon as it's profitable, I'm going to send you guys some money. It's best for all of us this way."

"That's what Mom said you'd say," I point out. "Except she didn't guess the rug cleaning."

My ghost dad looks irritated. "I guess she knows me."

"Then she said you like southern gals in Daisy Dukes."

He rolls his eyes.

I say, "Do you know how sad Nattie is you're gone? Do you know how much you hurt her?"

The ghost holds out his arm and vows, "You'll see me again."

"Don't give me any of that Ebenezer Scrooge horse-shit."

"I've got to go," says the spirit, and the weather grows heavy all around him.

"Dad," I call out. "Dad."

He is crying. "I'm sorry," he says.

"It takes a fucking hallucination to get you to tell me you're sorry."

"I'm sorry. I'm sorry. I'm so sorry." His voice is high and meepy, and it breaks my heart for an adult to sound that way, so broken, so desperate.

"I love you anyway," I say. The snow is getting heavier, and he is fading into the darkness.

He says, "You'll understand. I promise." And then, like it's the last thing he'll ever say, the figure says my name. "Adam. Adam." And, quietly: "You better go inside now. I don't want you to catch your death of a cold."

I will. I'm freezing. Snow is melting on my face. My temperature is down.

I leave him standing there in the driveway, clutching a prize – for me? for him? Who can understand the language of dreams? I close the door. When I look out through the window, he's vanished, of course, and it feels like something is over. Something has been settled.

Sleep is deep and restful, thick and delicious as caramel. I wake a few times to see that it's day. Once, Nattie is sitting reading by my side. I reach out and take her hand, and fall back asleep.

Later I wake up and it's almost evening. My mother is there. "Mom," I say. "I had another hallucination. I saw Dad." I smile. "He said he was sorry. He said he loved us."

"You *saw* him?"

"He said he's going to open a carpet cleaning business."

My mother nods sharply. She seems to be angry. "I know, Adam. I know. He left a note."

"It was a hallucination."

"No, Adam. Your father came by last night and apparently stole my car. The asshole still had a fob. He took the car and a couple of boxes of his stuff from the garage – old yearbooks and crap like that. High school trophies. He left a note saying he's selling the car to get some capital for wet vacs."

Nattie is standing the doorway. "Why didn't he come in and say hello to me?"

Neither my mother or I want to answer. We don't know what to say. Mom goes to Nattie and hugs her. I tell Nattie, "He said he loved you. Specifically. He said he was sorry."

But Nattie pulls away from Mom and walks out of the room.

In the evening, I do a pencil drawing of the driveway, empty. Snow is lying on the concrete. There are footprints there, leading up to a set of tire tracks, but everyone has left. The scene is deserted.

Stuffed Animals in a Line

The next day Hunter Marsh plays his music so loud I can't sleep. I pull myself out of bed and try jumping a few times on the floor, but he can't hear it or doesn't care. I'm desperate to fall asleep so the time will pass, and maybe when I wake up the news will have arrived that I have won a ticket to the next round of the human spawn art contest. So, wearily, I drag myself to Nattie's room and lie down on her bed and doze off.

When I wake up, I find her sitting on the floor, surrounded by all her stuffies. They're in lines like the military. She has a plastic crate and she's hurling them into it.

"Nattie?" I say. "What are you doing with Lulu? And Susan and Acre and French Fry and Up?"

She stops and answers joylessly, "I organized them."

"How? They usually go on your bookshelves."

"First by size. Then I decided to go by class of vertebrate."

"Nats, please: remember I have a fever."

"Like mammals, reptiles, birds, amphibians? Okay? Then that didn't work. It was too confusing with the squid and the horseshoe crab."

"Melvin and Slowpoke."

"So I'm doing it alphabetical." She resumes pitching the animals into the crate.

"Doing what?"

"Selling them. I don't care about them anymore. I'm too old for them."

"This is nuts, Nattie. You love your stuffies. They're your main collection."

Angrily, she says, "I'm thirteen. I have a boyfriend."

"They're going to feel abandoned."

"They're not real," she says. "They're cheap polyester filling. As you used to tell me again and again. When you wanted to make me cry." She picks up the crate. "I'm cleaning up my room," she says. "I'm selling them all. And if they don't sell, I'm throwing them all out." She leaves, and I hear her tromp down the back stairs to the garbage.

I lie there and I picture Nattie when she was one and a half or two; and her cheeks are crusted with old food, and she's holding out Up, who is also crusty with her food. She's offering me Up as a gift. Because he's the thing she loves the most.

And as strong as an ache, I want to take her in my arms and tell her the stuffies are real, my god, please, please, they're real. I want to beg her not to throw her childhood away. "They're your history in animals," I want to say, "and I love who you've been, and I love who you're going to be when you're older. So I love them."

But of course I don't. Why don't we say things to people? I go back to my bedroom to sleep, and then the Marshes are lurking around us when we're eating – stomping past up and down – and there never seems like a time to say any of it.

Then the day has passed and the mood has passed and it sounds stupid, because the stuffies are gone.

So instead, secretly, in my room, I draw them all. I sketch them in their rows, like the years of her childhood, Acre and French Fry and Lulu and Susan and Up and all the rest, organized alphabetically.

Someday I'll give it to her. When everything is better. The natural history of her life, sketched out, because nothing means as much until it has vanished.

THE LANDING SITE OF A
VUVV MEDICAL CLINIC,
BOSTON COMMON

"Ad?" my mother says. I have just woken up and I'm clammy with sweat. She holds up a letter. "A letter came for you. It's vuvv."

"It's the contest," I say. "Open it up!"

She's thrilled at the idea. She says, "Oh, honey, I can't wait," and she grabs my knees. I pull myself up in bed, leaning against the pillow. My arms quake.

"What percentage chance do you think you have?" she asks. "What chance of making it to the next round?"

"I don't know, Mom."

"Just a ballpark guess."

"Zero, if they want pictures of apples, sharp cheese, and oysters on the half shell."

She tears the envelope open. It's an official letter. I can

see letterhead with vuvv scratches through the paper. Then there are lines typed in English. I wait for her to give me the news, good or bad.

"Klieg lights and kick lines?" I say, coughing. "Or the big razz?"

She looks confused. "Oh, Adam," she says. "Adam."

I ask her what's wrong.

"It's that goddamned vuvv you worked for. It's suing you. Breach of contract, false representation, the whole thing. You're going to have to appear in court."

"Oh, no."

Mom keeps reading the vuvv brief. "Court date won't be till this summer. We have time to make a case."

"How?" I say. "We can't make any case. We don't have that kind of money."

My mother stands up with her mouth twisted and starts to crease the letter carefully between two fingers, as if she's going to tear it in three. Then I see her realize that she can't tear it. We have to keep the letter for its details. We can't even take the small revenge of ripping up their stationery.

Her arms bob uselessly by her sides.

I feel like I can't breathe. I start coughing.

"Honey," she says, "honey. We have got to find a clinic for you. A vuvv clinic. Sometimes they take cases on as charity."

When I can draw my breath, I wheeze, "That would be

great. Then I wouldn't cough out my intestines as well as shitting out my lungs."

"I'm going to check online. Maybe there's a clinic in Providence."

This is how five days later, we end up heading to Boston, where a clinic ship is landing for a day and taking patients for free on a first-come, first-serve basis. I go, even though I still have a fever over a hundred.

We don't have a car anymore, and it's almost a two-hour drive. We have to take a bus. I dodder down to the station with Mom as if I'm eighty-nine. I have to stop once to disappear into someone's bushes.

As I squat there miserably, feeling the cold on my ass, I call to her, "You know what's going to be great? A long, bumpy bus ride."

"Maybe they'll have a chemical toilet."

I stand up. "Better be some freakin' strong chemicals."

It takes us an hour to reach the bus station by foot. I have to just keep thinking of putting one foot in front of the other, as the old Rudolph Christmas special recommended. Houses pass slowly with dead bushes and the frozen corpse of snow.

The bus ride lasts forever. It costs us almost everything we have. My mother has been trying to get money out of the Marshes, but they aren't playing along. We don't have the money for legal proceedings to evict them. They just live there, furiously, in our house.

The bus drives up past the old brick factories of Pawtucket and Woonsocket. Finally, in the distance we can see Boston, where slender homes float above the glass towers. I shudder and minutes seem to take forever, and then the bus arrives.

A medical ship has settled on Boston Common. There are huge crowds around each of the doors. Hologram signs in vuvv float above each door, telling us where we should go, but no one can read them, so everyone just stands around confused. The ship is mobbed.

My mom drags me from crowd to crowd, asking which line is for gastroenterology.

Finally we find it, but it is long. The ship has been on the Common for two days, and people have staked out their places in line so they won't get bumped. They have tents or lean-tos or pieces of cardboard over their heads to keep off snow and sleet. As we wait, we hear that several people have already frozen to death.

Standing there for hours, I can only wish I would freeze to death. I don't know why we aren't allowed to just die when we want to. It seems very cruel to keep us alive.

"Draw something," says my mother. "Draw the ship."

I take out my sketchbook and a pencil.

"You know what's the worst line to stand in for days?" I say to Mom. "Gastroenterology. A whole line full of people who have to stand still but who constantly need to sprint for the shitter."

I am shaking so much, my landscape scene is electric with spastic motion. The houses of Beacon Hill are not stately in their rows. They are jagged, and the curve of the ship crackles with jitters.

Four hours later, we are thirty-five feet closer. The vuvv announce they are not taking any more patients. We are cheerfully told that there will be another free clinic in a month; to come back then.

By the time we get on the bus, the ship is already hovering above the Common, its lights reflected in the gold of the Massachusetts State House dome.

I hold on to myself during the drive back home. The bus jolts over the broken, unfunded roads. I close my eyes, but I'm in too much pain to sleep. I want time to pass, but time is always here, around us, not flowing, but static as thickening concrete.

MY HOUSE, UNDERWATER

(Digital media; unfinished)

I am very startled when my mother tells me our house is underwater.

I'm asking her, "Why can't we just move to someplace where there are more jobs? Why can't we just sell the house and go to, I don't know, wherever we need to?"

She says gently, "That would be a great idea, Ad, but we can't sell the house. It's underwater."

"What do you mean?" I squawk. I glance at Nattie. She just frowns. She isn't talking much these days.

"Not literally," says Mom. "It's nothing to worry about. It just means that right now our house is worth much, much less than what we paid for it. Back when your dad and I bought it, houses were going for way more. So we can't sell it right now, because we'd lose – I don't know – eighty thousand dollars, a hundred thousand dollars. We'd still be paying for it even though we didn't own it. That's called being underwater."

"Oh, thank god," I said. "I thought you meant there were eels in the den." I look at Nattie for comic support. Normally she'd start spinning fantasies about an octopus's garden and curtains of kelp and trout on the hassock but she's giving me nothing.

"Don't worry," says Mom. "The economy will get better. It always does. We just have to wait it out. The invisible hand of the market always moves to make things right." She holds up one hand like a fin or a sail. "To put things back on an even keel."

"The invisible hand of the market," I say.

Mom nods. "Markets always sort themselves out. It just takes some time. Values are relative."

"True in art, too," I offer.

"Ad, honey, please don't talk to me right now about art."

"It's true! Values are relative in art. Like light and dark. Mr. Reilly says in a dark picture, even gray can seem like light."

My mother thinks about it. She admits, "Okay, yeah. It's all in how you look at things, honey."

"Can't we declare bankruptcy or something?"

"It's not that easy. Especially not anymore. And especially with your father and me not being legally divorced."

"So we just wait for values to change."

"Exactly."

"And when the invisible hand waves, suddenly, the house won't be underwater."

"Bingo."

"Our life is a freaking dismal fairy tale. A maaaagical fairy tale."

That afternoon I paint our house underwater. I do it virtually; I'm sick enough that my hands tremble too much for brushes, and the smell of paint gives me a headache. Sketching in the air, I do the living room: a deep, sunken green, and a school of shad angles toward the landing. Everything we've known is cold and subaquatic, no longer ours.

I'm considering adding motion – like a VR fish tank, so you can watch species flit by for hours – when there's a ping and I have a message.

I halt the shad and check.

"Mom!" I yell out. "Mom, Mom, Mom!"

She rushes in, thinking I'm having another episode. A tangle of sunken living room surrounds me.

"I got it!" I tell her. "Nattie! I got it!"

The message flashes up. First it's in vuvv – but then English.

"'… delighted to announce…'" reads my mother.

"What is it?" asks Nattie, swinging around the door frame.

"Oh my god!" my mother exclaims, smiling. "Oh my god! He's got it!" Still reading, she grabs my face between her hands, grinding my cheeks in circles while calling out, "'... much consideration, you have been accepted as one of two teen finalists from the state of Rhode Island...!'"

"Are you for serious?" says Nattie.

"Yup, yup, yup, yup," I say. "Invited to have my work shown at the gala reception in orbit. A big shindig with all us visual artists showing our stuff and music by all the teen musician contestants. One lucky artist to get the fabulous award that night."

They hug me.

"I thought you had a sixty/forty chance of getting it," Mom says. "More likely than not. That was just my guess. I am so happy." She pats me on the shoulder and adds gently, "I just hope you can go."

I'm stunned. I wait for a second to figure out if she means what she says. "Huh?"

"You can't go if you're sick, Ad. It's in a few days, and you have a lingering infection and a temperature of over a hundred. You can't go up into orbit with that kind of fever."

"Mom."

"I'm not arguing, Adam. You realize that with your temperature, your life is in danger? Okay? Your actual life? We need to give the antibiotics a chance to work."

"Mom! It's my chance to leave Earth!"

"No, honey. No." She walks out.

I am furious. I shut my painting off. I am tired of living underwater.

It's time to dry this shit out, once and for all. I am going to leave this fucking underwater house behind.

SLOPPY SMILEY

(Mixed media)

Temperature of a hundred and four. In the early morning, delirium again: the line of people crowding through my room, judging my gut. But it's the day. The contest will be happening up in the sky.

My mother says with irritation, "You still want to go."

"Yeah. I'm going."

"No. Too sick."

"I've got to be there, Mom. It's our big chance."

"You going in an ironic Lil' Kim T-shirt and plaid boxers?"

"First of all, it's not ironic. I'm kind of a music historian. And for your info, I thought I could wear, um, one of Dad's suits. Since he's not going to be using them." She looks at me, sizing me up. "I could—"

"Honey. It's hard. I really want you to go."

"Yeah!"

"… This is our big chance. I know that."

"Right!"

"But you're not going." She strokes my cheek. "I thought maybe you'd be better by now. Maybe a twenty percent chance. But as it is, you could die if your temperature keeps rising. A fever of a hundred and four is really dangerous. So: out of the question. Sorry. No. Orbit is *prohibito*."

I nod sadly, for effect. Of course I'm going. I'll sneak out.

"And you're not sneaking out," she adds. "Got it? I'll be watching."

She goes out around noon, and while she's gone, I steal one of Dad's suits from the closet. I try it on. Roll up the legs so it fits. It's saggy around the middle. I'm skinny. I fold it and put it under my bed.

The shivers for most of the day. Huddled in bed, my teeth rattling. The time crawls. Then it's only a couple of hours until I'm supposed to be at a landing pad, preparing to lift off.

Mom is not kidding about watching me as evening approaches. Maybe she thinks I'm going to break down in tears because of lost opportunity. Maybe she thinks I'm going to be making a break for it. She sits in my room, reading. So I suggest we watch a movie together. "Mom, could you watch a movie with me?"

"Sure! What would you like?"

"*Thallium Dogs II: Assassin's Blade.*" She looks like she's going to protest. She hates action movies. "Mom, it's kind of a tough night for me. Please?"

So there we are, with high-rise combat all around us.

It works like a charm. Twenty minutes of laser engagement and detonating battle shuttles later, she's fast asleep. An hour and fifteen minutes until the lullaby of soft violence stops and she blinks awake. Now's my chance to make a break for it.

I stand up. I reel. My cheeks flame.

Carefully, I get into the suit, one wobbling leg at a time. I talk myself through each step of the plan, like I'm coordinating a heist with glass cutters, guy-wires, and suction cups. *I'm going to put my arm in here. Then the other arm goes in there. Then I'm going to drink as much goddamn water as my bladder can hold. Then I'm going to the garage, and I'm going to wheel my bike out onto the street. Then I'll put my right foot on the pedal...* It's starting to feel overwhelming.

"This ain't no welcome wagon!" bellows a hero – ah, the comfortable, stale repartee of the Hollywood paramilitary lock-and-load loner – and he opens up a noisy barrel of whoop-ass.

I tread carefully down the hall. I wish I could stop in Nattie's room, ask her for a good-luck kiss on the forehead.

129

But she would raise the alarm. I continue to the kitchen.

I drink all of our boiled water. The sick in the pit of my stomach is so strong I feel light-headed. I hold on to the counter. Next step.

I go into the garage. No cars. Just mounds of stuff. The light is already on. That's strange. I feel like someone is in the room with me, like I am being surveyed. My skin prickles.

Then I see them crouching behind some boxes, blanched in the fluorescents: Hunter Marsh and two friends. They are down on the ground, crab-walking like vuvv but paused mid-stride. They have frozen in place like cockroaches when the kitchen light snaps on. None of them have any hair whatsoever. They watch me warily, to see if I will mock them.

I go over and, with dignity, get my bike. The garage door rolls up into the ceiling.

I sling my leg over my seat and look back at the three men on the ground.

Hunter Marsh hisses, "Don't tell."

Their hands rasp against the cold concrete.

Hunter orders a language tutorial, "Start again!"

A voice floating in the air scratches a sentence in vuvv and then translates, "Is breakfast included with the double king-size room?" It repeats vuvv. I ride down the driveway, and the garage door lumbers closed behind me. I hear Hunter and his bros behind me clicking out their demands for alien hotel rooms they cannot pay for, as if they live in some kind of world where they are going out on the town and all the waffles will be free.

Then, pedaling. Streets dark, trees dead, snow flat. The road scarred with frozen slush. It is five miles to the vuvv launch site where the shuttle is coming down. I cannot imagine making it, but I cannot imagine giving up. After a mile, I'm wishing I could just wheel my bike into a shadow in the lee of some house and disappear. Become part of the darkness.

The effort is— And I hit a lump of frozen snow and spin out. Tumble onto the road. Slam. The earth is so hard.

First thought: suit's not torn. I lay my head back down on the pavement. Slowly, slowly I get up. Hands on my knees to make the joints work right. My teeth are chattering again.

A minivan has pulled over. A woman leans out a window. "You okay?" she asks.

"Okay?" I say unsteadily. "No ... not okay."

"What happened?"

"I have a fever of a hundred and four."

"Oh my god," she says. "Were you going to the hospital? Do you want a ride to the emergency room?"

I'm about to say no, about to tell the truth, about to wave her away, when I remember: on the way to the hospital, we'll pass close by the vuvv compound. The landing pad.

131

"Yes. Yes, please. Oh, you don't know what that would mean to me. I'm so sick and…" I am already opening the car door.

The minivan is driving itself. The woman sits in the backseat, with shopping bags of groceries around her.

I slam the door shut and lean my head back against the headrest.

"Your bike?" says the woman.

I confirm, "It's on the road."

She waits for me to go out and get it.

"I can't," I say. "Actually, could you just drop me at the vuvv business compound?"

The woman pouts. "Um, no. I'm not a taxi service."

"Hokey-dokey," I say. "Hospital, then. Please."

"Go ahead," the woman says to the car.

The car sets off. I look through the tinted windows at the grimy houses and the brown snow that pass us by.

The roads are hell. So many potholes, now that no one fixes them. Each time the minivan jolts, my head pounds, my stomach quivers, and I notice that I am groaning.

"I apologize for the uneven road surface," says the car.

"Just feeling a little under the weather," I tell it. "A little nauseous."

"You may mean 'nauseated,'" says the car.

"You know, Honda? Not all criticism is constructive

132

criticism." I clutch my belly and put my hand over my mouth. "Oh, god…"

The woman asks, "Is this going to be a problem, going forward?" She's clearly worried about the upholstery.

That's when I realize the way out of this car.

We're passing within a quarter mile of the vuvv compound. It's time for me to get out and walk.

I start with a few little deep gulps, try to breathe deeply. I retch for effect. "Whoo," I say. "Hmm. These windows roll down?"

The woman asks, "Are you feeling—"

"Not so good. In fact, really bad. Fever of a hundred and four, you know." I loudly bellow and then swallow.

"Maybe it would be better," says the woman, "maybe it would be better if you—"

"I'm okay I'm okay I'm okay," I insist, in just the kind of voice that shows I'm struggling to keep my shit together, and the woman yells at her car, "Pull over! Over!"

I launch myself out of the car and make a dive for the bushes. She thinks I'm going to stop there, but I just keep on running. I sprint into an alley. I think she realizes she's been had – I hear her shouting – and I feel a little guilty about it, because, after all, she did offer to drive me to the hospital, but I am due in orbit.

Then I'm making my way over paths across desolate

fields, with the lights of the vuvv compound in front of me. The paths are treacherous with clamshells of ice, and I'm slipping and stumbling. I have to pee; I drank way too much water before I left the house. I scramble onward.

Then there it is in front of me: the waiting area for the shuttle. There's a cluster of people there under the lights.

I have made it. I am going to my own art opening in space.

In celebration, I make art. While I'm still in the shadows, I piss a smiley face into the snow. There it is, though it takes some doing to shut off and on for the eyes. I may not win anything in orbit, but I still have made my mark upon the Earth.

And suddenly a spotlight falls on me.

I scrabble with my zipper.

The illumination is so bright, my arms have halos around them.

The shuttle is above me, flying to the landing pad.

Sweating, I cross over a border of wind-scorched weeds and step onto the platform.

The aliens have come for us, and we're ready to go.

A Vuvv Ship as Large
as a Small Town,
Up Among the Stars

We are taken up on a shuttle with kids from all over New England. Some people are tense and silent, and some are giddy and talk a lot. I am the only one pressed against a wall, quivering, watching the door of the bathroom jealously, like a dog guards a bone. This evening will be the music contest as well as the visual arts contest, so a lot of kids have guitars and the people in bands are all horsing around, psyching themselves up.

Outside the window, the Earth's mantle and the air drop away below us. I try to think about the distance between solid things; the color of the atmosphere. I am burning. I press my hand to my forehead. My hand shakes. My head hurts.

The vuvv ship where the American teen art nationals will be held is glittering with lights. We pour out into a throng of people from all over the country, and everybody is jabbering about how it's their first time off the surface. The husky scratching of vuvv announcements booms through the air above the shuttles, and those of us with translators lead the mob toward the innards of the ship.

My fever must be high. I can remember a bit of the art show. We're all pressed up against each other and swirling around in a circle. The judges have already decided, but we won't know who won until later, after the youth musicians play.

The huge gallery is filled with still lifes. Fruit, knives on the edges of tables, fish, bread, lobsters, flowers, and, of course, sneakers. They are labeled in vuvv and English. They're from all over the country and are of all sorts of things. Regardless, the vuvv have titled them all "Traditional Human Still Life."

There is my work: they have chosen the looted Stop & Shop, the vuvv compound rising out of the blackened suburb, Buddy Gui's Human Totem Mart, and, finally, my house in winter, with my father sitting on the stoop, his head upon his knees.

I am not the only one who tried to follow a path away from the still life, the dining room tables, the half-peeled oranges, and the rucked-up tablecloths. I see incredibly exciting work by artists my age who are trying new things, new forms: shifting scenes that float in front of the faux canvas; a statue with rows of faceless human shapes sitting while a saucer, vaguely vuvv-shaped, descends upon them; abstract cries for help, with holographic swings and limbs of color that jut out of the surface or plunge into the wall. Things I don't even have a name for – video sequences that hover over the floor, looming explorations of hovels where derelict families crowd the floors of old kitchens; a thing that appears burnt until you move, when it is whole. I wish I'd met these kids years ago and talked to them. Who knows what kind of art I'd be doing? I pray that I lose to one of them, one of the rule-breakers, not one of the sunny fruit piles, ho-hum plums, flat pdfs painted to order.

The music has started in the auditorium. Later I can barely remember this part of the evening. The humans sit on balconies, about a thousand of us. I choose a seat near an exit and a bathroom. I can tell I am white and sweating.

Endless fifties rock 'n' roll. "Now Dr. Touch and the Sensations will play the traditional human song 'Why Do Fools Fall in Love.'" God, that endless doo-wop sung by suck-ups with Brylcreem hair. I keep having to stumble out and go to the bathroom. Squat there, heaving – yes, I throw up, too – throw up the water I'm guzzling to keep hydrated. I go in and out – still songs about sweet little sixteen, hymns to some teen angel, all these goddamn cretins rockin' around the clock – in and out, in and out, while vuvv chaperones watch me. As I sit in a stall, crapping water, I think furiously that any one of those chaperones could pay to evaporate my syndrome for less than it costs them for their morning heap of exo-lichen. The shit people take for granted. It's unbelievable. All it would take would be one visit to a vuvv emergency room. They'd give me an injection or wave their wands or whatever they do, and I'd be free of infection.

Then back into the auditorium. Some bastard crooning that "All I Have to Do Is Dream," but translated, cannily, into vuvv, so it sounds like someone vacuuming shag carpet. In the prime seats below, the vuvv are going crazy. I close my eyes. Can't face watching time pass. Rockin' around the clock.

Then there's silence while a grand piano rolls out onto center stage by itself. A girl who was sitting near me in the balcony follows it out under the lights – scrawny, in a black dress that just hangs straight down. She sits down to play. She looks furious, like she hates everyone in the audience. I am, of course, instantly in love.

She starts hammering on the piano. I can't stand piano music, usually, and I have no idea what the hell is going on in the song, because there aren't any words or singing, but this girl clearly feels it, plays it as if she's cursing all of us through the keys. It's a fluttery sort of cataclysm. It sounds like utter collapse. To be fair, I get the sense that the song has parts that would normally sound pretty friendly, perhaps even happy; but this girl plays them like she's swearing at us all at the top of her lungs. Then it stops. She gets up and bows. Everyone is silent and confused. Finally, the vuvv make a polite rhythmic sound, and she walks off the stage.

While the next band plays some drivel about how they wonder, wonder (hoo-hoo wa-woo woo – *thump*) who wrote the book of love, I see the girl come back up to the balcony to reclaim her seat. I know I am not alone anymore. I have to speak to her. My stomach heaves, but I stand up. I am reeling, almost falling down, grabbing at a railing.

I sway in front of her. She looks concerned. I think, *Get a grip, chump.* I introduce myself to put her mind at ease. It doesn't go exactly as I planned. "My name is Adam Costello," I explain in a stage whisper, "and I have a fever of a hundred and four, as well as an ongoing syndrome that makes digesting anything living hell." Her eyebrows go up. I figure it is time to get to the point. "Okay, I don't really know you at all, not even your name, because I suspect that the vuvv announcer got it wrong, and that you're not really called Robert Schumann, but listen, Bob, there are a bunch of us up here who are confused and unhappy, and we don't even know why. Do you see the track I'm on? This contest is about us and celebrating us, but here we are, confused, and our own Earth's atmosphere is far below us, and we have got to stick together; we have got to clasp hands and tell each other, 'Thank god you did not paint another goddamn still life!' Thank god, Bob, and thank *you*, thank *you*, Bob, for playing whatever that insane crap was down there instead of 'Great Balls of Fire,' and by the way, by saying I want to clasp hands, I'm not being handsy, especially when you have fingers of flame I would not even want to touch. Wow, who knew DayQuil could ever work like this?"

She smiles politely, pats me on the shoulder, and then, averting her eyes from mine, squeezes past me to sit down.

I think, however, I've said my piece.

I go back to my seat. All I have to do is dream.

The concert is over. Next nightmare: reception. Milling. Cramping, headache. My fever must be through the roof. I wonder if I'm going to collapse.

Buffet on a table. My feet scrape. I've got to lean against a pillar. My god, they must have chosen the color of the cold cuts just to punch me in the stomach. I can't look.

Shirley with another vuvv. "Adam Costello. It's Shirley. This is my offspring Danielle. I gave all my spawn human names. I just think your names are so cute." I'm rocking back and forth, unable to answer, making gagging noises, so Shirley tries, "Here we are! Your big night!" Its scented spawn-paddles click as it shifts. "So how are you doing?"

"Sick," I say. "Running a fever. I am so sick, Shirley. Can you get me into a clinic? If you could just – it wouldn't cost you much – it's a syndrome I have that makes digesting food living hell. Shirley…"

It rears up slightly and backs away. "I'm sorry," it says.

"I wouldn't ask, except I have this vuvv lawsuit against me for faking sock-hop love, and it's going to cost so much we're never going to get out of the hole, and our house is underwater, and with this fever…"

"I'm afraid that—"

"No, look, okay, okay, I know this is weird, but really, Shirley, the treatment wouldn't cost much in vuvv money. You have got to understand, the difference between American dollars and vuvv ch'ch is so huge, you won't even believe how cheap the doctor will seem to you, because I'm telling you, please, the gulf between our currencies is deeper than the gulf between worlds, it's physical, it's metaphysical – vuvv currency is so strong on Earth it warps the space-time continuum, it sucks up matter, it's like economic antimatter, like a black hole, a black hole the size of a dime, the size of a single cent, okay? One tiddlywink, and I'd be cured. Shirley… It's great to meet you, Danielle. What do you do for work? Hey—"

But they have already moved away. Shirley does not even bother to think about the fact that I am wearing a translator when it rasps to its spawn, "Sorry, Danielle. It's so awkward when they beg."

I watch them clamber off. They disappear quickly in the

crowd, since vuvv are low to the ground. They're blocked by rockabilly tools in plaid shawl-collar blazers. I have got to get to the bathroom.

I sit there on a toilet for a long time, just trying to breathe. I wonder whether I actually took DayQuil when I was in the bathroom at home, or whether I accidentally swigged half of Hunter Marsh's Alopeesh-Sure. Stand up. Nothing left in my stomach. At the sink, I stop. Splash cold water on my face to bring down the fever. Pour the water down my shirt. It soaks my chest. Soothing! Out into the crowd again. Canapés. Seafood. Just looking offends me.

Then I see Robert Schumann. She's passing me with a Styrofoam plate full of baby carrots. "Ms. Schumann," I say. "I'm sorry."

"Adam Costello?" she asks. She points over to the wall, where my art hangs. I nod. She just pronounces, "Nice," but like she means it, or even means more than "Nice." She's looking down, either because she's shy, or because she has noticed I poured cold water down the front of my shirt. My tie is out of whack and my shirttails are hanging out.

"Bob," I say, "let me explain. I owe you an explanation." I take a deep breath. My big chance. "By 'a fever of a hundred and four,' you understood I meant Fahrenheit, right? Because I would hate to think..."

"My name's Lucy," she says kindly, pulling away. "Maybe

we could talk when your temperature is below a hundred."

"Fahrenheit."

"Fahrenheit. Or at least Celsius."

"You are right. I am burning up. I am *burning the hell up.* Whoof!" I fan my cheeks.

There is a rasping over the PA system. The judges are about to announce the winners of the art and music contests. "Listen!" I say. "Lucy Bob – you have my vote. You were amazing."

"Thank you."

"That was a great song. You should win. Completely."

She smiles briefly, but she is working her way away from me.

"Bob," I whisper urgently to her back. "Bob, wish me good luck."

She turns briefly and her eyes are fully on mine. We're two people looking at each other fully. She says, "Luck."

Then she makes a pretty definite move away into the crowd.

"All right," I mutter. "That was a little noncommittal, in terms of good or bad luck, but it'll have to do."

And then the announcements start. A vuvv emcee is going to declare the winners. It's making an opening speech. I cross my fingers as the scratches that echo through the hall are translated in my earbud, with a little interference from the sound of people shuffling uneasily or scraping plastic forks across Styrofoam, which of course all means something accidentally in vuvv. "... until now, your species has always hoped to climb to the heavens through art – and now a select few of you will. 'To the stars through struggle!' We vuvv have long respected human hope, even when it seems foolish or..." I can't listen to this. I head back into the bathroom to splash my face with more water.

In the mirror, I look like a dead man. My face is almost green. There are dark circles around my eyes. The sink is too fancy to drink out of.

I go back out. More vuvv talking. Vuvv introducing other vuvv. *Could not have been done without the help of. Would like to thank. And also here tonight is the Vice President of Stteetchh Extraction, Inc. He will say a few words to. The kind support of the Vuvv Co-Prosperity Alliance Council on Interstellar Arts.*

I sit down on the floor.

All the young human spawn I see here tonight. To be seen across the worlds, by species circling more than thirteen suns. Tremendous hope, is what I'd like to.

I wonder if it would be rude to lie down.

I hear clapping. Human clapping. Someone is being called up: the winners of the music competition. It's not Lucy Bob Schumann. She didn't stand a chance. I can't see the winning band and I don't remember them. Apparently they sang an ironic twist on traditional human comedy song "One-Eyed,

One-Horned, Flying Purple People Eater." Really. Sent to other worlds. Singing "Flying Purple People Eater." Our message to the universe: *I like short shorts.* I've got to go back to sleep.

More clapping. Art. Hanging in space above the judges. I can't see the judges over the crowd, perhaps also because I'm lying down. Third place. They're announcing third place... *In the United States Nationals for Young Human Artists of...* I stumble onto my knees. Everyone goes wild. It's a still life. Seashells on a rumpled tablecloth. All right, good for him. Her. Whoever. Clapping.

Second place. *So thrilled tonight to award.* I can barely keep my eyes open. Applause. It's a still life. Huge, three-dimensional, in space. Plums, one half-eaten. One held in the arms of a wooden Oaxacan jackal puppet. It's a sweet-looking kid who's crying with joy. Okay. You deserve it. You have your own story.

"And now for the winner..." I really need to go to the bathroom. Stomach rumbling. "Now, for the... We would like to ask a young man named Adam Costello to come up in front of the audience."

And I can't believe it. Adam Costello. It is me. It is me. Applause. Applause all around me. There is one of my landscapes projected into the air.

Speech? What if I have to give a speech? I think about everything I learned about writing essays in high school, which are kind of like speeches. Unfortunately, the English class was taught by vuvv tech, which didn't have much of a reason to care whether we could write five-paragraph essays or not. The applause has died down.

Overwhelmed by possibility – suddenly giddy. It is incredible. My family will get what we need. A break. Somehow, finally, a break. No debt. My mother will be proud. Just this speech to make, this little speech, and then they'll hand me the envelope, and so, gathering my courage, only weeping a little, I begin.

"Since the beginning of time," I start. "Since the beginning of time, the *Oxford English Dictionary* has defined 'still life' as a painting of some stuff, fruit or what have you. But sometimes, don't you look at a still-life painting and think, *Hey: Is this still life?* Emn? Eh? If you don't quite get my meaning, ladies, gentlemen, vuvv – remember that I do at the current moment, on this night of all nights, have a temperature of a hundred and four. That's Fahrenheit. Screw Celsius. Hey, even these squat little empire-builders can't get us to go metric – *AM I RIGHT, AMERICA?*" There is not the welcoming roar I am expecting. In fact, there doesn't seem to be any motion at all.

I continue, "I have not come here tonight, ladies, gentlemen, and vuvv, I have not come all of this way, leaving the Earth's atmosphere far behind me, to convert Fahrenheit to

Celsius, which is almost as difficult as converting American dollars to vuvv ch'ch – because, in the end, there is a greater gulf between Fahrenheit and Celsius than between the planets. It's important to look at the quality of the air between things. When you look at exchange rates, as we do, every day, since we are paid in dollars and we spend, essentially, in vuvv cash, we must ask, *What does it mean? How do numbers stand for things?* Like health and nutrition? And yet they do, up here, above the clouds, stand for things, ladies and gentlemen and others. Money is only money because we pretend it's money. Worth something. Worth other money. Dollars and pesos and rupees and vuvv ch'ch. We perform value like a play. We know the script. Just like, my fellow dreamers, we perform love, because we know what love is supposed to look like. So we perform it for each other and think it's real. But – and here I quote – I wonder, wonder, hoo-hoo wa-woo woo, thump, *who wrote the book of love?*' Who, huh? These are difficult questions, people, and I will try to answer them all in order, thank you very much, sir or madam, and may I say you are looking fertile tonight, no, really, fecund enough to bud twelve kids. And if you convert that to Fahrenheit, that's twelve kids plus thirty-two, times one point eight – or no – twelve times one point eight, plus ... – *Am I right, America...?*"

It is really starting to sink in that no one is listening to me. It may be because I have not budged from my spot, so

I'm still standing in the middle of the crowd, and my translator horn is not being amplified. One of the vuvv is saying over the PA system that they don't know where I am, but that they are greatly indebted to me.

"Here!" I say, raising my hand. "Present and accounted for!"

"Because," they say, "it was through this painting, this landscape by Adam Costello, that we discovered the marvelous work of tonight's winner: Buddy Gui."

I lower my hand. I am a little confused. Buddy Gui?

"After seeing Adam Costello's painting, we sought out Buddy Gui, whose marvelous, powerfully primitive work is depicted in this simple plein air scene. And we found the incredible Mr. Gui carving *this*, with a crude gasoline tool, in preparation for Christmas."

My painting fades. In its place is the 3-D image of a rough-hewn Virgin Mary and Child, except the Virgin Mary is swaddling on her lap (silent night, holy night) an infant with the head of an elephant.

I poke someone standing next to me. "Excuse me," I say in an undertone, "I have a fever of a hundred and four. Fahrenheit. But is that a combination of Jesus Christ and the Hindu god Ganesh?"

The guy next to me hisses to shut up, freak, and he's not going to say it again. The judge is saying that what Mr. Gui has captured in his fabulous sculpture is the love between a parent and a parent's spawn, something no one understands better than the vuvv. There is nothing more important. This statue records one of the oldest human myths, the story of the Virgin Mary – the only human to bud like a vuvv. And the judge tells us all the story we all are supposed to know, about how there was no room at the inn so Mary laid the babe in a manger, and then Joseph came in and was sore angry because he didn't know who the father was, so he cut off the child's head. And then he repented what he had done, and promised he would go into the jungle and find the first head he could find, and put it on their child's shoulders, and make him whole. And he went out foraging in the deserted places, and lo, an angel of the Lord came down, and brightness was all around him, and the angel said, "Be not afraid." And there was an elephant caught in a thicket by its tusks...

"Oh, come on," I say. Then there's Buddy Gui, coming up in front of the whole audience, and all the vuvv judges are going crazy. Blaring praise about how here is the true human artist, the artist who conveys the essence of spiritual human values, and there shall be a Virgin and Child like this in every corporate boardroom from here to stars known to humankind only by number.

My stomach sinks. I have not won. Our last hope, gone. The debt settles on me again. The impossible debt of paying back the vuvv for fake fifties romance – thousands. And also, the cost of vuvv medicine. It is on my shoulders again. Lights are flashing. Nausea passes through me in waves, like a green sweep of the rendering sails through night. I have to sit. I grab on to the guy next to me. He almost slaps me before he sees I'm fainting.

Dim sense of safe. On the floor. I see Lucy Bob's worried face.

Close my eyes. More peaceful this way.

Everything in my ears is hissing, which might be vuvv or just collapse.

Pulled – yanked – though wish to lie still. The voices of human and vuvv.

The gurney lifts. Lights too strong; then none. (Vuvv like dim.) "... above standard human body temperature. Danger of enzymatic..." and then the translator box is ripped off me and I can no longer understand the clicking.

Awful pressures. "Not in my mouth – no, don't..." Then gag.

Safer to sleep. Lights again, bright through my lids. Finally, though, I manage: gone.

A Small Town
Under the Stars

When I am fully conscious, I am sitting on a concrete slab beside the high, glowing lights of the vuvv compound. I cannot believe how cold I am. Perhaps it is because I am wearing nothing but a hospital johnny. Next to me, neatly folded in a plastic bag, are my jacket, my pants, my shirt, my tie, my plaid boxers, and my ironic Lil' Kim T-shirt. I dimly remember that I crapped myself again, though it was mostly water.

I see the shuttle lifting off from the compound. *Okay,* I think, *maybe I didn't win anything, but at least they washed my clothes.*

I get up, sore all over, and start doddering barefoot for home. After a few burning steps, I sit down again. I pull my shoes out of the bag. I put them on. I stand up and start walking.

After a time, it occurs to me that I have the rest of my

clothes. Maybe I will stop and get dressed. Maybe tomorrow, I will look up the evening's program and check out the full name of a Lucy who played piano. I will find her and send her a message in a low-key, normal sort of tone. For the moment, I walk, freezing, through the town under the stars. Distantly, the rendering sails wash back and forth, a borealis yielding some mysterious benefit to our business partners and guests.

Perhaps I will paint this town – from a distance, as if it is on a far hill – and in the foreground, an enclosure of gold, a secret garden, a retreat in which I am safe. I will hide there, and the hand of god will wipe all tears from our eyes; there will be no crying, neither will there be any more death, because the former things will pass away. The invisible hand that guides our deeds, our acts, our markets, will not be able to touch me there. Outside of space and time, time and space, there will be no distance between ourselves and what we wish for; no infinite gulf between currencies; the gulf between currency and eternity is great enough.

The sky above me glows like the ancient patina of saints.

My House in Early Spring

(Final Rendering)

When I wake up from my long, strange dreams, there is sun in my room. I have slept for a long time. I sit up.

It hits me: I don't have a fever. I am not delirious. There is light in the windows and across the floor. I raise my arms and lower them. I take a deep breath. My head feels clear for the first time in weeks. My eyes are focused. There is no buzzing in my ears.

When I collapsed, the vuvv in the emergency room must have healed my infection. I remember, vaguely, being close to convulsions. They must have given me something for the fever. Maybe the Merrick's? Too much to hope for. I get up – still steady on my feet. I jump a few times in place. Still good. No dizziness. I run down the hall to the kitchen to tell my mom the good news.

When I got in late the previous night, having sneaked out with a fever of a hundred and four, there were angry words. A lot of shouting. Accusations of me being selfish, crazy, cruel. My mother sobbing. I asked her how *Thallium Dogs II: Assassin's Blade* ended, and she had to restrain herself from slapping me across the mouth.

But now I am full of health – health and an idea so large, I am brimming with it. I slide into the kitchen on my socks.

"Mom!" I say. "I'm better! No fever! The vuvv healed me!"

She is sitting at the table examining screens. She raises her eyes to me slowly with the menacing gaze a J-horror *yurei* might level on their guilty victim. Apparently we are not quite over our little tiff of last night.

She asks venomously, "What are you talking about?"

"When I was out, they must have injected me with something or run me under a scanner or whatever they do. I think the infection's gone."

"Really?" She says it cautiously.

"And I have an idea. It came to me when I was asleep."

"This should be good. If it's anything like the ideas you have when you're awake." She's by my side and feeling my forehead with the back of her hand. "You don't have a fever. It's a miracle."

"It's not a miracle. It's vuvv meds. Let me get Nattie. I'm about to blow your minds."

I go knock on Nattie's door. "Nattie. Nattie. Nattie. Everything's clear to me."

She comes out. "Did you win?"

"No! No, I lost, Nattie. Your brother lost. That's how I got this amazing idea. Come on."

We are gathered together in the kitchen then, all that's left of our family, and I can't hold back my idea any longer. "You know what our problem has been for the last couple of years? You know what it was?"

"I could name a few," says my mother.

"Shhh! The problem is that we keep on trying to win. Hell, we're American. We keep on being surprised that victory isn't ours. But this is what I saw last night, with a temperature of a hundred and four, standing in that crowd: *the secret of moving forward right now is losing*. Our real problem is that *we haven't lost enough yet*."

"This is not a good idea," says Nattie.

"It is! The house is underwater. There are no jobs here. We're about to be slapped with a huge vuvv lawsuit for fake love. We need to start again. We need to leave this house, leave this town, leave this state, and begin with nothing – because zero is more than negative something."

They look at me like I'm crazy.

"I was standing there in that crowd, a loser, and suddenly I saw it: nobody pays attention to the losers. You can say anything you want as a loser. People are looking in the other direction. They only pay attention to the winners, or to people who are still in the race. If we drop out – disappear – change our names – go someplace else – we can start over."

"You seem real peppy," says Mom. "Do you think they cured your Merrick's Disease? Or just the infection and the fever?"

"Doesn't matter, Mom! Because if I still have the Merrick's? We just take me to a paying clinic and get me the necessary vuvv treatment. Heal it completely."

"That will cost—"

"Have them send the bill here. Who cares? We'll be gone. This won't be our house anymore. The bill will come to your old e-mail or through the slot in the door, and it will just sit there. I'll be healthy and we'll all be in Colorado or somewhere, with me selling paintings and you – I don't know, Mom – whatever you want to do!"

"This is a ridiculous fantasy."

"Whose name is on the house's mortgage?"

"Your father's."

"So if we disappear...?"

Now they're starting to think about it. I can tell I've almost won when my mom murmurs, "I wonder where you can buy fake Social Security numbers?"

"That's the spirit, Mom! *We can be losers.*"

Now I sit outside in my coat in the afternoon. The temperature is up close to fifty, and everything is melting. I'm painting what might be my last version of this house with its shingles and panels. Hunter Marsh peers out the basement window at me, like a troll. I paint him in.

I enjoy his irritation at being painted in. It's my family's house, after all. At least for the moment.

Forty-five minutes or so after I start working, Chloe comes home. She has just been out with Buddy Gui, apparently. She is popping the vuvv hookup nodes off her forehead and shaking out her hair. Apparently she has made a new deal for sponsorship.

"Beautiful day," I say. Sometimes optimism is the best offense. "Can you smell the spring in the air? The winter is just melting away."

She decides to sneer. "So Buddy won," she prods. "Your big, interplanetary art contest. You thought you were great, but he beat you."

"The gutters are running clear."

"He's going to sell his statues all over the galaxy."

"Day like this makes you feel like a million bucks." I give an exaggerated sigh of contentment.

"Yeah. Buddy's going to *make* like a million bucks."

I turn and really look at her. I wonder whether I should include her in the painting I'm doing. And it's weird: she looks just the same – beautiful – but somehow different. Just a person. I can't understand how I was attracted to her. Why did I want to kiss that face? How was it possibly so important to lock those fingers in mine, to slide my hands up to those breasts?

She's not special to me. I'm not special to her. There is no way I'm going to include her in the last portrait I do of my family's home. We are already absent from each other. We have left each other, and there is an impossible distance between us.

It is as if my body is already gone. As if it has already packed a couple suitcases and a backpack with my important things, and it has fled in the wet night with Nattie and Mom, Nattie giggling like a prankster as we leave the only house we've ever lived in. As if we are already sitting on a bus, Nattie asleep with her head on my arm, drooling on my sleeve. As if the house is already empty behind us, with the furious Marshes squatting there confused, uncertain of whether to be rude and triumphant or stunned and suspicious, waiting for the bank to seize the property and evict them.

I am already in a new place, driving toward a new horizon.

"You think you're so great," says Chloe. "You're *no one*, Adam. You're *nothing*."

I laugh politely. "No, Chlo, I'm less than nothing," I point out. "I won't be no one without a little hard work."

I paint no shadow in the spot where she stands.

AN UNDISCLOSED LOCATION
IN THE BLUE RIDGE MOUNTAINS

This is where we got off the bus. Mom has a job as a waitress in a spa town, the kind of place where rich people like an actual human in an apron to serve them chocolate pie and call them "Hon." Nattie will start high school here in the fall. I'm a few months short of a high school degree, but I have a portfolio of landscapes now, both virtual and painted, and I'm going to make a business out of painting wealthy people's houses. "Here's your place floating over Asheville on a day when the clouds are as gentle as dolphins." I would paint portraits for them, but Mr. Reilly has admitted that my noses never work.

The apartment is not large. Nattie and I have to share a bedroom, two mattresses on the wood floor. There's only one bedroom, so Mom sleeps on the living room couch. "That's fine," she says cheerfully. "I don't get home from my last shift until after midnight anyway, when you guys are in bed. We don't need a whole house. It's great we can live so compact." Nattie and I creep around like kittens in the morning so we don't wake her up. We close the door softly when we go out into the daylight.

I contacted Lucy shortly before we left the old life behind. Now we send each other messages. I told her our house was underwater. She recorded a piano song about a cathedral engulfed by the seas and sent it to me, full of dim, chiming bells and green gloom.

I call her from the public library. We can't actually afford a connection in our apartment yet. It takes a while to build yourself up from nothing.

"Heya, Lucy," I say.

"Heya, Adam."

"Not Adam anymore."

"You had to take a false name."

"I guess you think that's kind of a red flag in a guy."

"After you fled your state."

"You know, Luce – you know, at a certain point, when a guy is holding up enough red flags, he's just speaking to you in semaphore."

The mountains lead down through the heights. The air between them is blue. Ships arrive from other stars, tracing lines of credit and expense through the skies, constellations of commerce. We sit on the porch in the evening and listen to the insects chitter like the fever of our drained, exhausted Earth. Orbital stations glimmer in the last light.

We thought there was a great distance between the future and us, and now here we are, falling through it.

Nattie closes one eye and raises her hand in a lazy finger-gun, as if to shoot the vuvv and the hovering wealth out of the sky. Someday, things may fall, and things may rise, but for the moment, we sit on the porch and wait.

We are tiny figures, pointing at wonders, provided for scale, no lives of our own, surveying the landscape that has engulfed us all.

M. T. ANDERSON is the author of *Feed*, winner of the *Los Angeles Times* Book Prize, the National Book Award-winning *The Astonishing Life of Octavian Nothing, Traitor to the Nation, Volume I: The Pox Party* and its sequel, *The Kingdom on the Waves*, both of which were *New York Times* bestsellers and Michael L. Printz Honor Books. He is also the author of *Symphony for the City of the Dead: Dmitri Shostakovich and the Siege of Leningrad*. He lives near Boston, Massachusetts.

Turn the page to read an extract from
M. T. Anderson's award–winning novel

FEED

"We went to the moon to have fun, but
the moon turned out to completely suck."

Titus doesn't think much of the moon. But then Titus doesn't
think much period. He's got his "feed" – an internet implant
linked directly into his brain – to do his thinking for him.

Then Titus meets Violet, a girl who cares what's happening
to the world, and challenges everything Titus and his friends
hold dear. A girl who decides to fight the feed...

awake

The first thing I felt was no credit.

I tried to touch my credit, but there was nothing there.

It felt like I was in a little room.

My body—I was in a bed, on top of my arm, which was asleep, but I didn't know where. I couldn't find the Lunar GPS to tell me.

Someone had left a message in my head, which I found, and then kept finding everywhere I went, which said that there was no transmission signal, that I was currently disconnected from feednet. I tried to chat Link and then Marty, but nothing, there was no transmission signal, I was currently disconnected from feednet, of course, and I was starting to get scared, so I tried to chat my parents, I tried to chat them on Earth, but there was no transmission etc., I was currently etc.

So I opened my eyes.

college try

"Nothing," she said.

I had gotten up and was sitting on a chair beside her. We were in a hospital. We took up a ward.

Link was still asleep. Nurses went by.

I said, "I can't see anything. Through the feed."

"No," she said. "Or through my hospital gown. So stop trying."

I smiled. "You know, I thought maybe . . ."

"Sure you did. Want some apple juice?"

We'd been up for fifteen or twenty minutes. Everything in my head was quiet. It was fucked.

"What do we do?" she asked.

I didn't know.

boring

There was nothing there but the walls. We looked at them, and at each other. We looked really squelch. Our hair and stuff. We had remote relays attached to us to watch our blood and our brains.

There were five walls, because the room was irregular. One of them had a picture of a boat on it. The boat was on a pond or maybe lake. I couldn't find anything interesting about that picture at all. There was nothing that was about to happen or had just happened.

I couldn't figure out even the littlest reason to paint a picture like that.

still boring

Our parents had been notified while we were asleep. Only Loga hadn't been touched by the hacker. She hadn't let him touch her, because he looked really creepy to her, so she stood way far away. There were also others, people we'd never met, who had been touched, and they were in the wards, too. He had touched thirteen people in all.

There was a police officer there, waiting in a chair. He told us that we would be off-line for a while, until they could see what had been done, and check for viruses, and decrypt the feed history to get information to use against the guy in court. They said that they had identified him, and that he was a hacker and a naysayer of the worst kind.

We were frightened, and kept touching our heads. Suddenly, our heads felt real empty.

At least in the hospital they had better gravity than the hotel.

missing the feed

I missed the feed.

I don't know when they first had feeds. Like maybe, fifty or a hundred years ago. Before that, they had to use their hands and their eyes. Computers were all outside the body. They carried them around outside of them, in their hands, like if you carried your lungs in a briefcase and opened it to breathe.

People were really excited when they first came out with feeds. It was all *da da da, this big educational thing, da da da, your child will have the advantage, encyclopedias at their fingertips, closer than their fingertips, etc.* That's one of the great things about the feed—that you can be supersmart without ever working. Everyone is supersmart now. You can look things up automatic, like science and history, like if you want to know which battles of the Civil War George Washington fought in and shit.

It's more now, it's not so much about the educational stuff but more regarding the fact that everything that goes on, goes on on the feed. All of the feedcasts and the instant news, that's on there, so there's all the entertainment I was missing without a feed, like the girls were all missing their favorite feedcast, this show called *Oh? Wow! Thing!*, which has all these kids like us who do stuff but get all pouty, which is what the girls go crazy for, the poutiness.

But the braggest thing about the feed, the thing that made it really big, is that it knows everything you want and hope for, sometimes before you even know what those things are. It can tell you how to get them, and help you make buying decisions that are hard. Everything we think and feel is taken in by the corporations, mainly by data ones like Feedlink and OnFeed and American Feedware, and they make a special profile, one that's keyed just to you, and then they give it to their branch companies, or other companies buy them, and they can get to know what it is we need, so all you have to do is want something and there's a chance it will be yours.

Of course, everyone is like, *da da da, evil corporations, oh they're so bad,* we all say that, and we all know they control everything. I mean, it's not great, because who knows what evil shit they're up to. Everyone feels bad about that. But they're the only way to get all this stuff, and it's no good getting pissy about it, because they're still going to control everything whether you like it or not. Plus, they keep like everyone in the world employed, so it's not like we could do without them. And it's really great to know everything about everything whenever we want, to have it just like, in our brain, just sitting there.

In fact, the thing that made me pissy was when they couldn't help me at all, so I was just lying there, and couldn't play any of the games on the feed, and couldn't chat anyone, and I couldn't do a fuckin' thing except look at that stupid boat painting, which was even worse, because now I saw that there was no one on the boat, which was even more stupid, and was kind of how I felt, that the sails were up, and the rudder was, well, whatever rudders are, but there was no one on board to look at the horizon.

ENJOYED THIS BOOK?
WE'D LOVE TO HEAR
YOUR THOUGHTS!

🐦 @_MTAnderson
@WalkerBooksUK
@WalkerBooksYA

📷 @WalkerBooksYA